NINTH
EVOLUTION

MD JOBE

ISBN: 978-1-966343-32-5 (hard cover)
ISBN: 978-1-966343-33-2 (soft cover)

Edited by Erika Nein

Published by Warren Publishing
Charlotte, NC
www.warrenpublishing.net
Printed in the United States

To my wife and children—you inspire me every day

PROLOGUE
Central Africa, Early 1840s

The sun starts to peak over the horizon, casting long shadows across the arid ground. The thin shadow stretches out in front of the tired miner returning home from a hard night of work. His feet scrape along the ground, raising a slight plume of dust in his wake.

"Papa!" yells a small girl as she runs out of a modest shack to meet him en route.

"My sunshine is up with the sunshine," he teases as she hugs him around the waist.

"Do you have anything for me to work on?" she asks eagerly.

The father reaches down and removes a flap from the sole of his shoe. "I was down in the lower tunnels last night and was only able to pick up a few samples," he says, handing her some small pieces of metal crusted with dirt. "Do you have your brushes ready to clean them off?"

"I do!" she happily replies. Taking the metal, she sits on a nearby rock with a makeshift brush crafted from a stick shredded at one end.

The man enters the house and greets his wife and two small boys, who are eating breakfast. He sidles up to the sink to wash up as his wife puts a plate on the table for him. He nods toward his daughter outside. "Did she get some food this morning?" he asks.

"Yes, of course," his wife replies. With an amused look in her eyes, she adds, "She wants to be up and ready when you come home. She thinks it is her job, that she is helping the family."

"She is a joy," the man says as he sits. After inhaling a few bites, he shakes his head irritably. "I don't think this new tunnel I worked in last night is safe," he tells her around a mouthful of food. "The airflow was terrible, and the support structure did not look stable."

As they begin to discuss his concerns, the boys noisily rise from the table, thrust their dishes into the sink, and rush outside to play.

The wife sighs tiredly. "We'll finish this conversation after you get some rest," she says, then follows the kids through the door with an armful of dishes to wash at the river.

After a few hours, the man is roused from his sleep by a crashing of dishes just beyond the front door.

He peeks outside, shielding his eyes from the bright midday sun. As his vision clears, he sees his family all slumped over on the ground near the spot where his daughter had been cleaning off the metal samples.

"No!" he yells, running to his wife's side. She is breathing but unconscious. He quickly checks both of his sons, also breathing but unconscious. As he gets to his little girl, the man starts to feel lightheaded. He leans in to check her for signs of breathing, and collapses.

The sun is setting when the man finally regains consciousness, awakened by a woman's scream.

He quickly looks around and sees other members of the village covering their mouths with cloths and backing away from him. He sees his daughter is also coming to, leaning on her elbow, staring at the ground behind him. He turns and sees his wife and two boys have not opened their eyes. Frantically, he lunges toward his wife, pulling her into his arms. All signs of life are gone. He checks on the boys and lets out an agonizing cry that echoes throughout the village.

The villagers flee, fearing the spread of a deadly illness. After some time, the shattered man rises from his knees and begins to solemnly place the bodies of his family in the house. The daughter, in shock, almost robotically sweeps up the metal pieces and the pile of dirt she cleaned off of them. The father tells her to hide them in the house so nobody will know he pilfered from the mines. They fill two small sacks of belongings, then he cleanses the area by setting the house on fire. He takes the hand of his daughter, and they begin to make their way to the coast in search of a new place to live.

Within a few days, they are picked up by a group of slavers and held in a pen near the port for two weeks before being loaded onto a ship bound for America. At least forty other men and women are crammed into the bottom of the ship's hold with them, but the father soon distinguishes himself as one of the strongest and most tireless workers. The ship's captain comes to rely on him to lead and communicate with the other slaves. The young girl also proves to have great stamina and strength and is quick to pick up the English language. She is often chosen to work with the ship's own slave girls, tending to the crew and keeping the ship clean.

The night before they reach the port of Charleston, the crew—relieved at the successful crossing of the ocean—break out some bottles of rum, and a rowdy celebration of dancing and horseplay sweeps across the deck. One of the men leers lasciviously at the girl as she tries to clean up the deck. He gets to his feet unsteadily, then takes a last swig before tossing his bottle to the side. He staggers over to the girl and grabs her from behind. She shrieks as he throws her over some crates and tears at her clothes. The father hears her cry out, instantly recognizing his daughter's voice, and uses all his strength to bust open the door of the hold and race to the deck. He is on the crewman in seconds, pulling him off of his daughter. Spinning him around, the father takes but an instant to tear out the neck of the crew member, then drops his lifeless body to the deck. As he leans over to check on his daughter, multiple gunshots ring out. The man's chest bursts open, and he falls limp over the dead crewman.

To make a statement and prevent further unrest, the crew wastes little time in censuring the girl. They take her up to an elevated front deck and tie her small body to the mast. The first bites of the whip rip long crevices across the girl's back. She is strong and makes barely a peep as the crack of the whip echoes in the cold night air. It takes over twenty lashes before she hangs motionless, the ties around her wrists the only thing keeping her body upright.

"Get some sleep, you lot!" commands the captain, who was drawn to the deck by all the ruckus. He eyes the dead slave. "Shame to lose such a fine specimen. He would have fetched a pretty penny at the auction," he comments as the crewmen clean up and toss the male bodies overboard.

***

It is bright and sunny in the morning when the ship docks to unload the slaves. The captain pauses as the last crew member starts to depart. "You stay on board and clean up that mess left on the upper deck," he says, motioning to the mast with the girl still hanging off it. The man goes right to the galley and yells for one of the ship's slave women to clean it up. Then he crashes down on some tarps in the shade to recover some of the sleep that he lost the night before.

One of the women grabs a mop, some towels, and a bucket before climbing to the upper deck platform. The sun is shining brightly across the deck as she unties the rope, allowing the girl's body to drop to the floor. She uses a rope to lower the bucket over the side of the boat to scoop up some water. Then she throws the water along the deck boards and over the blood-soaked body. She begins to mop the floor first before attempting to throw the body overboard, saving the heavy work for last. The water splashes on the girl's body as the mop sweeps back and forth. Lines of water run down the girl's back, revealing smooth and already-healing skin beneath the dried blood. Curious, the woman steps closer, running her finger along one of the lines of water. She starts to pull back as she feels the girl take a breath, but the girl is lightning quick as she spins over, grabs the woman's wrist, and yanks her down. A small startled scream escapes before the girl can cover the woman's mouth.

The crewman below wakes with the sound of the scream and hurries to the upper deck. He finds the woman standing in front of the mast, still clutching her mop, held from behind by the girl whose fierce eyes blaze at him through a tangle of ravaged hair.

"What the fuck!" he yells, stepping toward them. He lashes a backhand across the woman's face, launching her from the girl's grasp. The girl catches the mop as the woman falls to the deck. Taking one step forward, the girl jams the back of the mop handle through the man's right eye. The force of the upward thrust lifts his whole body off of the ground before it crashes lifeless to the deck.

The girl stands frozen for a moment, staring at the body as her mind flashes back to the death of her father the night before. Her head snaps to the side of the rail as she hears the woman crying and mumbling to herself.

"Haki ya Lisa. Haki ya Lisa."

The girl's face crinkles, briefly wondering why the woman is calling her the daughter of the sun god, then realizes how much danger she is in. Once again, in her short life, she's on autopilot. She grabs the woman's rope and ties it to the mast, then steadily lowers herself into the water. Swimming with a frog-like stroke that she learned paddling in the rivers near her village, the girl quietly crosses the harbor waters to an outcropping of land just south of the boat. She climbs up the shore and stands on a small rise of land looking back over the harbor. The blood washed off, replaced by the dripping of sweat and water, she sees the bustling Charleston waterfront for the first time.

CHAPTER 1

Those same eyes now look out over the Charleston harbor from the other side of the wharf as the van cruises over the Ravenel Bridge. The woman always thinks back to that day nearly two hundred years ago, when she first set foot on this continent. How her life has changed ... She looks at the two young people sitting next to her—held still by the forces she exerts over them. *They are just starting their journey*, she thinks. *Could their change be the sign that the time has come for the next evolution?* Her concentration is yanked back to the present moment as the van swerves and a horn blares from one lane over.

"Dude, what the hell are you doing?" yells the front-seat passenger, grabbing hold of the oh-shit bar above the window. "That's not our exit!"

"I'm hungry," replies the driver. He gives an apologetic wave to the car he almost ran off the road. "There's a McDonald's off that exit. I was going to swing through the drive-through—"

"But we're almost there," the passenger interrupts, gesturing at the road ahead of them. "And you *had* to stop at Bubba's 33 earlier today. You had three burgers and some onion rings. You will survive."

The driver utters a disappointed groan. "I always go to Bubba's when we're near Gastonia," he quibbles. "It's my thing ..."

"Please," says the other man, shaking his head, "just drive."

Decklan and Lauren sit quietly in the middle row of the van, listening to the exchange between their two captors in the front. The small Black woman sits behind the driver, next to Decklan. He can't quite see her—his head is frozen, looking straight ahead—but he can hear her shallow breathing.

Dek has been listening to her breathing and the men's bickering for the past three hours, ever since he and Lauren were kidnapped in Charlotte. Dek is dying to check on his partner, who is sitting to his right, but both their bodies are being held immobile. He knows their current predicament has something to do with the story he and Lauren had been about to go public with: the accident in their Madison lab, the virus that caused physical changes to their cells, that maniac Vince, the explosion in Chicago.

Lauren has been amazing through this whole ordeal, Decklan thinks. *She's probably already planning our next move even though we can't actually move.*

After only a few more minutes of the men arguing about the driver's insatiable hunger and the passenger's flawed taste in "spa music," the van pulls off an exit ramp. Decklan actually agrees with them both; he is also very hungry, and the music *was* kind of calming during the stressful ride.

They drive through the center of downtown Charleston, passing the college area and the touristy Market still bustling with shoppers and sightseers. They move slowly along the path toward the Battery, an area known for its beautifully colored row houses and historic battle sites. The van slows and turns into a small, one-car garage located at the bottom of a large, old house a few blocks away from the main tourist areas. The garage is very plain, with cinder block walls and an antique wooden door situated directly in front of the van. The engine goes silent, and everyone sits quietly waiting as the garage door closes behind them, shutting out the sunlight and leaving only the glow of the fluorescent tube lights positioned along the ceiling. The van starts to shake and then smoothly descends into a lower parking area. They park in one of the six spots, three of which are already occupied by a variety of other vehicles: a sports car, an older Model T, and a row of three motorcycles. The van stops and both the driver and passenger turn toward their companions in the back seat.

"Home sweet home," says the passenger. He points to Dek and Lauren. "I know this is crazy for you two, but we need you to be cool. Our lady friend here is going to let you go. We do not want to fight you. We are actually here to help you, but we can't have you getting all scared and causing someone to get hurt." He pauses, looking at them for a sign of acknowledgment. "Both of us are currently armed, but we don't want any trouble. Again, we are here to help you."

The back driver's side door slides open, and the older woman gets out. Her cane makes a soft tapping sound as she slowly walks around the back of the van toward a door at the end of the parking area. She pauses a moment and waves her right hand in a circular motion before continuing on.

Decklan and Lauren collapse forward onto their laps.

"Holy shit," says Decklan, between panting breaths. He gently places his hand on Lauren's shoulder. "Are you okay?"

Lauren sits back in the seat, looking up at the ceiling and catching her breath before refocusing on the men staring back at them. "That really sucked," she says, trying to stretch her arms over her head. "I hope you boys are telling the truth," she huffs, still a little out of breath.

"If you two are going to be cool, can we go in and get some food now?" the driver asks impatiently.

Dek and Lauren get out of the van slowly. It takes them a minute to get their bodies working right again.

"What did she do to us?" asks Dek, shaking out his legs.

"I don't think anyone really knows how Urvinder does that, but it is very effective at avoiding a fight," replies the driver, slamming his door. He nods his head. "Head on over to that door on the far wall."

There is a large window next to the door, and a small woman with short black hair and glasses glances up from her computer screen, then buzzes them in.

"These two seem calmer than the last group you boys brought in here," she quips as they all walk past her down a short hallway.

The walls are old cinder block and smell a little funky to Dek and Lauren. They both wrinkle their sensitive noses and peer around until they are directed to a room on the left-hand side of the corridor. They enter through a solid metal door with a square of thick glass in the middle, about a foot wide.

The two men wait for them to enter, motioning them to sit at an old table with two desk chairs on one side and a folding chair on the other. "Someone will be in shortly with some food."

Decklan and Lauren wait for the men to exit before saying anything. She reaches for Dek's hand as the door closes and they hear it click locked.

"Well, I guess this is a step up from the dark storage closet," Decklan jokes, referring to the basement room Vince locked them in at the lab in Madison.

"I think it's safe to say they can probably hear everything we discuss in here," Lauren says, starting with a word of caution. "But, seriously, what the hell just happened to us?"

Dek shrugs and glances around the prisonlike room. "I guess we should be getting used to things like this by now: being kidnapped, shot at ...." He notices surveillance cameras in two of the corners and gives them a little wave.

"Yay, our new normal," Lauren says sardonically. "Though, I'm not getting the same sense of fear here as in the lab closet. I hope these guys are on the good side of all this. I mean, the driver is definitely the cop from the hotel who saved us from getting killed by Vince. Did you notice that?"

"Yeah," Dek says. "But they still grabbed us and brought us here without our consent." He stands to stretch, slowly rolling his head back and forth and side to side. "I don't get a really bad vibe either, though ...." He swears under his breath when his neck cracks. "But what is up with that old lady, Urvinder? That was insane how we weren't able to move for the whole trip."

"Come here," Lauren says, gesturing for him to sit in front of her. "The way they were talking, it sounds like Urvinder may be one of the leaders here." She gently massages Decklan's neck and smiles when he groans appreciatively. "I would definitely feel better if we—"

Before she can finish the thought, they hear the click of the door locks. A small Black man pushes the door open with his back, coming into the room with a tray.

"Ahh!" he says cheerily as he sets the tray on the table and removes the protective domes from the food. "My new guests, you are finally here." He steps back from the table and motions for them to eat.

Lauren and Decklan both stare at him. Recognition slowly dawns on their faces.

"Please, eat, eat," the man pleads. He sits down in the folding chair and smooths his khaki pants. "You must be hungry from the long drive."

They are both, in fact, starving and, after a conspiring glance, dig into the spread in front of them. Minutes go by in silence as they eat and glance back and forth between each other and the small man.

"Blue windbreaker ... in the park in Chicago," Lauren finally says in between chews.

Pointing a finger at the man, Decklan nods in agreement. "Yeah, you were the buzzing guy that we saw near the fountain."

"Yes, my friends. So nice of you to remember, but I guess you remember just about everything these days," he says excitedly. He holds out his hands and they can hear the same humming, or buzzing, sound that they first heard a few weeks ago.

"What *is* that," asks Lauren, "and why didn't you sound like that when you came in here?"

"All of us sound like that," he says, his slight French accent becoming a touch more pronounced. "It is the sound your cells make when they are working at this advanced level. You should hear what you two sound like to me." He puts his hands up to his ears. "Two Newbies, you are buzzing like a swarm of bees."

Lauren's data-driven brain shifts into higher gear as she considers this information. "Then how come I can't hear Decklan?" she asks.

"You have been around each other so much, your cells are in sync, so it probably just sounds normal," the man patiently explains. "Once you have been trained, you will know how to quiet your cells. That way, others will not find you so quickly, unless you want them to, like in the park …."

Lauren narrows her eyes. "Wait, so you purposely allowed us to hear you in the park?"

"Yes, my friends. It is a fun way to test a Newbie." He grins sheepishly. "If you were not changed, you would never hear the sound of another person's cells."

Decklan follows the conversation but continues to devour his food. Around a mouthful, he says, "The scientist in me really needs to hear more, but this food is really good." He pauses mid-chew and raises an eyebrow. "Wait, you wouldn't be giving us our last supper or anything, would you?"

The man laughs with delight. "No, no! I am glad you like the food. I made it special to welcome you, our newest friends."

The door to the room swings open, and the driver of the van walks in. "I hope Frenchy didn't talk your ear off and actually allowed you to eat," he says.

As Decklan nods, Lauren looks at the small man quizzically. "Really? Your name is Frenchy?"

That brings another bout of laughter. "No, no. My name is Darley Blake, but most people here call me Frenchy. I am the librarian slash historian of our little group. I also do a lot of the cooking. You can't live in Charleston and not eat good food," he says with a quick wink.

"What group—" Lauren starts, but the driver interrupts her.

"You'll find out soon enough," he says, motioning for them to finish up. "Come on. It's time for your information session."

Decklan takes a giant last bite while Lauren balls up her napkin and throws it atop her plate. They walk into the hallway, followed by the driver holding the door for Frenchy, who slides through sideways with the food tray.

"Killer burger," the driver says to Frenchy, offering up a quick fist bump.

Decklan turns around and cocks his head. "Didn't you have, like, three burgers already today?"

The driver snorts. "I basically eat like a beast all day. Judging by the way you just took down that tray of food, you do too. I think we're going to be good friends, bro," he says, slapping Decklan on the back.

The group rounds a corner and finds a small golf cart with four seats in the larger hallway.

"All aboard," the driver says. "Let's get this shit show on the road."

CHAPTER 2

The golf cart takes a slow, smooth ride along the dimly lit corridor. Every thirty feet or so they pass a door or a glass-paneled room marked by an antique gaslit sconce hanging on the wall. The total trip lasts only a couple of minutes.

The hallway seems to slope downward slightly as they near their destination. The trail ends in a small roundabout with a regular-sized door off to the right and a heavy wooden door, at least ten feet tall and adorned with intricate carvings, at its center. The cart comes to a stop in front of the large door.

"I'll see you in there," Frenchy says as he hops off.

Decklan catches a glimpse of steel kitchen shelving and a commercial stove as Frenchy shoves the food tray through the smaller side door.

The driver is standing next to the larger door, beckoning them to follow with an impatient hand wave. "Let's go, kids."

Decklan slides out of the seat. He offers Lauren his hand to help her out of the cart. "I think you're up next on the tee box," he quips.

She rolls her eyes as she takes his hand. "Golf humor?"

"I mean ..." He gestures to the golf cart and grins.

They barely have time to examine the carvings on the door before it opens, but Lauren manages to catch a few images: a large depiction of the sun and two men standing at the head of a group of people so big that it seems to fade off in the distance; it reminds her of the sea of people in a concert crowd.

They enter a massive circular room with at least twenty-foot ceilings. Their eyes are immediately drawn to a round table at the center of the great room. There are two large chairs at either side of the wooden table and a series of smaller chairs completing the circle. The walls are lined with bookshelves overflowing with weathered books and scrolls. A metal torchlight adorns the ends of each shelf, casting a dull hue of light and giving the impression that the shelves disappear as they fade back from the main area. An enormous glass-blown chandelier—a burning sun with giant rays emitting from a multicolored center—hangs high over the table.

"Wow," whispers Decklan as they enter the expansive space. "Now I know why we were descending on our drive over here. They needed more height for this room. It reminds me of my uncle's basement library—minus the brown-paneled walls, plywood bar, and excessive Packers' decor."

Lauren just nods, still trying to take in the existence of this massive room beneath the homes of Charleston. "We never had anything like this; mine was more, like, unfinished, with a sports goal and Ping-Pong table," she replies.

They both straighten up as they notice other people materialize out of nowhere from the shaded sides of the room. It must be a visual effect of the chandelier's light, hiding others not seated at the table.

"Ahh, our new guests have arrived," says a tall, thin man standing in front of a large chair. With dark shoulder-length hair, dark eyes, and skin tanned from the sun, he is elegantly attired in a burgundy-colored dress coat; the woolen fabric of the coat hints at a more casual look.

"He looks like a character out of a Victorian vampire movie," Lauren mutters to Dek, who coughs to cover his laugh.

"I am Alexander," the man declares. He walks over to shake their hands and bows slightly to Lauren. "It is so nice to meet you both." He motions them toward the table. "Please, come and join us; we have much to discuss."

Decklan and Lauren take two of the smaller chairs closest to the door. Alexander sits on the opposite side as five other people come forward, seemingly out of the walls, to take seats next to him.

"I'm here. I'm here," calls Frenchy, breaking the tension as he scoots through the door. He grabs a seat next to Lauren, giving her a slight pat on the hand as he sits.

Alexander gestures to the tall, muscular African woman to his left. "This is Thi Thi Ungwé, my personal assistant. Next we have Carson Waller, who has been driving you around, followed by Philippe Laforge, who also accompanied you from Charlotte."

Decklan keeps a watchful eye on the older woman Alexander presents next, leery of her ability to immobilize him.

"This is our elder stateswoman, Urvinder Gurm, who has some very unique talents and helped us bring you here safely and without conflict." Alexander then nods to the short, dark-haired woman from the computer room. "Maria Espironza. She handles our computers and technical equipment." He finishes with an elaborate sweep of his hand to their side of the table, as if he were doing introductions at a society party rather than a kidnapping. "And I believe you have already met Frenchy, our mother hen."

A lull briefly settles over the table until Lauren leans forward in her seat and directs her gaze at Alexander. "I guess it's nice to meet you all," she says, "but we were brought here against our will and still don't understand what is going on or who you people are."

Alexander nods slowly. "I do apologize for the method in which we brought you here, but I assure you it was for the best." He sips his tea, then gently places his cup on the table. "We are the Children of the Sun. Like you, we have evolved due to what we call the 'evolutionary virus.' I have personally studied the effects of this virus for over a hundred years, having contracted it in 1913 while on a—"

"Wait, what?" Lauren blurts out. "You're saying you are over one hundred years old? But ... you look, I dunno, maybe fifty?"

Alexander raises an eyebrow. "As I was saying ... I contracted the virus while on a dig in Africa with seven others. The virus quickly entered each of our bodies and changed our DNA, only two of us for the better. I and one other survived; the others quickly developed an aggressive form of cancer ...." He pauses to let that sink in before continuing. "As I have come to understand it, the virus is a key to evolutionary leaps in the progression of the human species and other forms of life on Earth. I have spent much of my life learning everything I can and looking for others who have been changed before the next true leap."

Decklan raises his hand, feeling a little like he's back in grade school learning about science for the first time. "I'm afraid that I may need a little clarification about what's going on here. This sounds very close to what we had theorized in Chicago, but can you explain what *you* mean by 'next true leap'?"

"Of course," Alexander says. "You see, we are the rare cases to have encountered small bits of the virus ahead of the next evolution. We believe that at some point the virus will be released, causing— in one single leap—the next significant evolution of man. I refer to this next phase as an awakening of our cells, increasing the body's cellular ability to function on a higher level."

Dek bobs his head in excitement. "Yes, Lauren and I have some, uh, interesting new abilities!" He scans down the table. "Does this mean she and I will continue to develop crazy powers, like Ms. Gurm—" He stops, suddenly distracted by the new person seated to Urvinder's right. "Wait. Who's this guy?"

Only minutes ago, Philippe, the maybe-thirty-year-old handsome man who had ridden shotgun with them all the way from Charlotte, was seated next to Urvinder. Now there's a man in his fifties with graying temples, wrinkles, an additional twenty pounds, and a week of beard growth.

"Always joking around, Philippe," Alexander says with a slight laugh. "Not everyone will have the gifts that Urvinder and Philippe have developed. It takes many years of work to achieve some of the amazing things that your bodies are now capable of. Philippe often takes the lead in surveillance when we suspect that someone new has encountered the virus, because he can drastically alter his appearance in just a matter of minutes—"

"Or even seconds," Philippe interjects with a confident smile.

"As for Urvinder, she will never share her secret of how she can immobilize people with but a word, but I guess if you're almost two hundred years old we can cut you some slack," Alexander continues.

Both Decklan and Lauren shift their dumbfounded gazes to Urvinder, who tilts her head slightly in acknowledgment.

"We think we may have touched on this in our experimenting, but can you clarify how, or why, you are all living so long and hardly aging?" asks Lauren, turning back to Alexander.

"When the virus gets into your system, it very quickly changes your RNA, allowing it to read greater sections of your DNA," Alexander says. "If you have the correct gene makeup, your cells will become 'smart cells'. This cellular change allows those cells to heal themselves, resist infections, and function on higher levels to respond better to your needs." He points to both Dek and Lauren. "You have seen this in your own bodies ... your compatible genes enabled the virus to evolve all of your cells. Our DNA has always held the ability to fully evolve our species to its highest level. Our RNA, the part of this process that reads the DNA code, can only read the portions of the strand that are appropriate for our current level of evolution. Each viral evolutionary leap changes how the code is read and which genes are expressed."

"Hopefully, your science backgrounds will help you understand the complicated process that Alexander likes to throw out like he's discussing the weather," Thi Thi says in a buttery voice, bringing a tinge of humor to the intense conversation.

Lauren and Dek are quick to nod.

"I think we are following along as well as can be expected," Dek says.

"We have so much to learn," Lauren adds. "Like, how is the sun involved in all this?"

"Ah," replies Alexander, glad to see that they may be further along in discovery than he previously thought. "Did you pick that up from the name or your research?"

"A little of both," replies Lauren. "We knew that the sun in some way was causing or helping with the changes we were going through; 'Children of the Sun' kind of clinched it."

"You are correct, on both counts," Alexander replies. "Our name is in reference to something Urvinder was called many years ago when she first came to this continent, 'daughter of Lisa'—Lisa being the African sun god, of course." He clears his throat. "It has long been a belief in this country that sun exposure is bad for you, causing cancer and skin discoloration. But this is only an effect on the unevolved. The sun is the center of our solar system and the main reason that this planet can support life at all. It is also an important catalyst to the process of evolution. When the sun's rays fall on either the inactive virus or on the skin of someone infected by the virus, the virus becomes active within the body ... and highly infectious. Many of the people who initially take in the virus but do not have sun exposure may have hours or even days without the virus becoming activated by the sun."

Dek soaks that in for a moment and nods. "When the virus is fully activated," he asks with a quick glance over at Lauren, "can the sun cause the person to lose consciousness?"

"Yes—"

"I knew it," Lauren exclaims, lightly banging her fist on the table.

"But that usually only happens when the infected person has come in contact with the actual virus. It would be less likely in the case of your friend, who was infected secondarily from your contaminated blood," Alexander points out.

"Huh?" Lauren shoots Decklan a questioning look. "What do you mean 'our friend'? We never infected anyone else with our blood."

"Your friend Richard," Carson says. "He had end-stage cancer when Vince shot him at the hotel. He probably would not have survived the morning regardless, but the swiftness of his body's decline could have only come from the virus."

"Richard had the virus?" asks Decklan, shaking his head in disbelief. "We never gave him a sample …. He asked me about it, but … shit, that idiot stole some from the lab and injected himself?"

Lauren rests her hand on Dek's shoulder. "You couldn't have stopped him. He was dead set on finding some kind of golden ticket to riches," she whispers quietly.

Carson agrees. "Based on some of the last searches on his computer, it did appear that Richard was going to try and market his blood as a kind of miracle cure. He had no idea that he couldn't infect anyone with his blood-borne viral load, though."

Again, Lauren and Decklan are surprised by this revelation.

"Wait, so he could get the virus from our blood but was unable to infect anyone else from his own infected blood?" Decklan asks.

"That's correct," says Alexander. "Only the blood of a person who is directly infected by the virus can cause the evolution to occur. We refer to people who have been secondarily infected as the Blood Borne. They still have the same chances that the virus will become cancerous and kill them, but their blood cannot create another Blood Borne evolution. We think it is due to the decreased viral load—"

Alexander is cut off mid-sentence as the tablet resting on the table in front of Maria lights up red and starts buzzing. At the same instance, the watches of every member of the Children of the Sun sitting around the table start to buzz.

Maria looks up urgently from her tablet. "Cleo just activated her mini-EMP. She's only a few blocks away, at the end of the Market."

"Shit! That can only mean one thing," says Alexander, abruptly standing and knocking over his tea. "You boys take the bikes; we'll follow in the Jeep."

Carson and Philippe rush out the door, tearing down the hallway. Alexander and Thi Thi follow quickly, running for the garage area.

Maria, Frenchy, and Urvinder have a furtive conversation, then the women exit through a side door. The three remaining in the room turn to look at one another.

"Never a dull moment," says Frenchy, shrugging his shoulders. "If you two would please follow me, we can take the elevator to the upstairs library, where I'll give you some private time to digest everything."

CHAPTER 3

Seven minutes earlier …

A large black Suburban pulls off the highway, following the same path that the van traveled earlier that day, continuing through the historic Charleston downtown toward the Battery. The driver looks like a sardine squished in a can, even driving such a large SUV. His enormous right hand casually engulfs the steering wheel, and his head bops slowly to the smooth jazz playing on the radio.

"Man, I love this song. Babe, what do you think?" he asks in a thick Australian accent. After a few seconds without a response, he reaches up to shift the mirror. "Hey, Cleo! What do you think of this song?"

Sitting behind the passenger seat is a short, athletically built woman with long, brown hair cascading around her richly tanned shoulders. Cleo is rolling a small gold cross necklace between her fingers as she stares intently at her phone. She briefly glances up as she sees him shifting in his seat. "What, babe? I'm watching videos on my phone," she replies loudly with a crisp Colombian accent. "You have to speak up."

The man quickly glances back, seeing the buds in her ears and realizing she isn't hearing any of the music playing through the car. "Never mind. You know no one can talk to you with those things on?" he shouts. Red brake lights ahead pull his attention back to the road. "Shit, there shouldn't be this much traffic on this road at ten o'clock," he complains as he brings the truck to a complete stop. They are about a block from the traffic light that sits at the end of the downtown Market. "I thought we were making good time."

The woman looks up and stretches to see out the front windshield. "Babe, the traffic shouldn't be this bad at this time of night," she shouts, not hearing his previous comment. "What's going on? Can you see?"

He shifts his hulking shoulders to shoot a look at her.

"What?" she asks defensively, raising her hands, then pulling out one of her buds.

"I just said that same thing," he mutters, then decides it's not worth the argument. The traffic starts to move forward slowly, one car at a time. "Okay, I think we're starting to go. It looks like there is a cop up there directing what little traffic there is."

They are two cars from the intersection and Cleo once again shifts forward to get a better look at what could be the problem. "Something's not right, Brutus. There are barely any cars for the cops to direct. Why are we creeping up so slowly?" She sits back in her seat and lowers a computer keyboard out of the back of the passenger seat.

The truck that is two cars ahead of them turns right, stopping at the corner and clearing their vision of the intersection. There is a lone cop with his back to them. He is tall and lean, wearing a blue police hat and a black trench coat with the word *Police* across the back. He raises his left arm, signaling a car to cross the intersection, and the sleeve of his coat drops down his forearm, revealing a tattoo that looks like a snake wrapped around his arm but is really a double helix strand of DNA.

"That's not a cop, that's Anubis!" Brutus yells, then hastily pushes some buttons on the middle console. The middle partition slides open and two silver handles rise up toward the driver's seat armrest.

"Shit! They must think we have the package," says Cleo, quickly typing away. A similar console to her left slides open, raising the stock of a compact FN Minimi submachine gun.

The sedan in front of them is directed across the intersection, moving them up. The cop still has not turned around. Brutus glances around, scanning the intersection. "We have a lot of walkers to the left and the truck that was ahead of us is still sitting at the corner. What's our play?" he asks, urgency breaking in his voice. He slides one of the handguns into a holster under his left arm.

"We are so close. Help will come quick, but will it be quick enough?" she asks, both to him and herself.

He pulls forward that last length of car, coming to a stop at the intersection, and puts the truck in park. There are not many cars at the intersection, but Anubis has perfectly positioned them to prevent Brutus from just plowing through.

"I'm releasing the mini-EMP and opening the roof. They must be after the package. If they see we don't have them, they may leave us be." The sunroof of the truck rises up out of the roof. It is specialized with bulletproof glass and steel risers on the back sides. When it locks open about two feet above the roof of the truck, a small disc fires out of one of the supports like a bottle rocket. It pops about forty feet above the truck, giving off a surrounding crackle of sparks. All of the electronics for five city blocks go dark.

Cleo grabs her gun and jumps up, planting her wedge sandals on the arms of the backseat captain's chairs. She pops out of the roof, aiming her gun toward Anubis across the intersection. Her light-blue sundress flaps across her legs as Brutus opens the window on his door. Keeping the gun in his left hand aimed out the open window, Brutus reaches across his body to open the door. Easing out, he uses the door as cover. "What's happening, mate? Long time no see," he yells out.

With his left hand still up in a motioning position, Anubis's head snaps to the right, revealing his pointy nose and hard-jawed profile. A wicked grin creeps across his face in anticipation of what's to come.

"Is that you, Bru?" Anubis asks slowly in an Australian accent, turning toward the intersection. His coat billows open and reveals a submachine gun draped around his neck. "Old friend, it's good to see you. I see beautiful Cleo is still faithfully by your side."

"We don't have what you're looking for, mate," Brutus says blithely, keeping the gun trained on Anubis through the window. "No need for a dustup."

Cleo shifts to her right to cover multiple approaches. "I've got the truck. Watch the boys near the bar on your nine," she cautions. "They must be Newbies; they're buzzing like a swarm of bees."

"You know I can't just take your word for it," Anubis calls back in a casual, friendly tone. "Why don't you two lay down your guns and go get a draft at the pub—"

Before he finishes his sentence, the four men standing near the bar to the left of the Suburban charge forward with evolved speed. At the same instance, the back of the truck stopped on the corner to the right slides open and four more men jump out, sprinting for the black Suburban.

Cleo rapidly shifts her aim to the right, sending a spray of rounds across the legs of the men from the truck. Three are down with the first volley. The first of the men from the bar is closing in on them. Brutus fires two rounds toward Anubis, forcing him to leap out of the way. Brutus then clenches his massive right hand into a fist and, punching across his body, nearly takes the head off the first man attacking him. The man's head snaps back, slamming down on the street. The next two men dive across his fallen body to pin Brutus against the side of the SUV. One is holding his left hand against the door frame while the other is attempting to tackle him to the ground. Brutus manages to duck as a shower of bullets slice across the front of the truck and the driver's side door.

Anubis has recovered his balance and lights up his own gun. "Whoo! Feels like old times, doesn't it, mate?" he yells over the pops of expelled rounds and a flood of expired casings cascading to the ground.

Cleo is forced to retreat down into the Suburban as the bullets just miss her perch. "Bru, are you okay?" she yells down into the truck. She pops back out of the roof and returns fire on Anubis, this time forcing him to dive for cover over a parked car. The last man who emerged from the truck, having managed to dodge Cleo's bullets, jumps up and grabs Cleo's gun. She slashes a knife-hand chop directly to his throat, smashing his esophagus and causing him to drop from the truck, clutching his neck.

The fourth man attacking from the driver's side diverts to the back of the truck, carrying a briefcase-sized box. He slams the box against the truck to activate a screen on the underside of the device. "Shit!" he says, analyzing the display. "They're alone!" he yells over the commotion. He taps his watch. "They're alone!" he repeats, shouting into his wrist.

Brutus launches his knee up under the man restraining him, lifting him three feet off the ground and knocking the wind out of him. Regaining his full footing, Brutus grabs the neck of the other man restraining his shooting arm. They lock eyes for a split second, before the man loses consciousness under the viselike grip of the behemoth.

Another spray of bullets from Anubis forces Cleo and Brutus to dive back into the truck.

"Did you hear the distant hum of motorcycle engines?" Cleo yells over the sound of bullets slamming into the hood.

"Cavalry is on the way!" Brutus shouts back, lying across the front seat. "Just need to hold out a few more minutes." He reaches his left hand back outside the driver's window to return fire. A motorcycle lights up its engine from the direction of the Market, but, Brutus can barely get his head out of the way as another stream of bullets showers down from the left, slicing into his beefy left shoulder and thrusting him across the driver's seat.

An older dirt bike model of motorcycle comes careening down the steps of the Market. It must have been parked just out of sight along the side. A woman with a mane of dark curls and blazing brown eyes lets out a screech of delight as she fires round after round into the driver's side window. The bike thuds as it reaches the street, skidding up next to the Suburban. She kicks up the throttle and speeds forward to where Anubis is still firing on the sunroof perch.

"Time to go already, my love?" asks Anubis as she pulls up next to him. "I was having so much fun with my old friends."

"I think we had better go before we are outnumbered," she replies, scooting forward in the seat. He jumps on the back, spinning the gun around under his coat. The bike skids for two feet before speeding down the street. More men rush out from the sides of the intersection, quickly gathering what's left of the attackers into the truck that was parked on the corner. The back of the truck slams down as two more cycles speed into the intersection.

Carson and Philippe open fire on the truck as it pulls away from the corner, following the dirt bike. They get to the black SUV as a Jeep pulls up to the scene.

"Is everyone okay?" yells Alexander, jumping down from the Jeep, astonished by the bullet-riddled Suburban and blood splattered all around. He gets to the driver's side door and looks in, seeing Cleo's small frame clutching Brutus's head, her hand trying to stop the blood rushing out of his shoulder.

Alexander just shakes his head. "Time to go."

It takes all four of them to get Brutus's six-foot-five, three-hundred-pound frame from the shot-up SUV to the Jeep.

CHAPTER 4

Decklan and Lauren don't actually get their private library time. All the excitement immediately draws Frenchy into the computer control room with Maria, and he allows them to stay and observe the tech genius at work.

Her fingers flying across the keyboard, Maria first generates a fake accident call to the police, drawing the department's attention out of the downtown area. Then she tracks the huge firefight in downtown Charleston by hacking any passing satellite imagery of the area. Lauren and Dek, grateful not to be locked up down the hall, sit quietly and exchange wide-eyed looks.

Maria interprets the activity for them between hacks. "What you didn't see is that Cleo's mini-EMP deactivated any security cameras in the area and, of course, any cell phones nearby that could have recorded the fight," she explains.

Minutes later, Maria laughs. "And that should get rid of most of the evidence left at the intersection," she says when they watch Alexander push a button under the Suburban's steering wheel, causing a fire.

She swivels around in her seat. "Okay, they'll be coming back now, and it looks like Brutus was badly hurt. Let's get ready. Frenchy, get a gurney to the garage level. Urvinder, if you could prep the surgical area? You two come with me. There may be a way for you to help us in this situation."

They all rush to different parts of the facility. Decklan and Lauren go with Maria to a small room next to the room Urvinder is getting ready. It is small and very clean and looks just like a doctor's exam room with a patient table and two chairs. There is a cabinet and counter space located in the back corner.

Frenchy rushes past their open door, pushing a gurney back toward the garage area. "'Never a dull moment.' How could I have jinxed myself with that line?" he murmurs to himself as he goes by.

"Okay, I am going to need a blood sample from both of you," says Maria as she digs through a drawer, pulling out needles and vials and placing them on the counter. "Go ahead and have a seat."

Decklan and Lauren exchange curious glances as they sit down on the chairs placed along the wall.

"You do know that our blood is not normal?" Decklan asks lightly, patting the inside of his elbow and causing his vein to show.

Maria wheels over on a small stool. "All of us have evolved blood," she says, pulling a rubber strap around his arm. "You two were changed less than a month ago so you have more of the active viral components in your blood than any of us. We call you recently evolved 'Newbies.'"

A low hiss escapes Decklan's mouth as Maria inserts the needle into his arm like a pro, quickly filling up five vials of blood. "Your blood will hopefully stimulate Brutus's cells to heal faster," she says, patting him on the shoulder. "I think Brutus evolved sometime in the 1950s ... old-ass blood." She smiles at her own small joke, scooting her stool over to Lauren.

"Were you a nurse?" Lauren asks as Maria, again, expertly draws Lauren's sample.

Maria nods. "All of us here hold multiple degrees. Extended lives and perfect memories set up nicely for higher education. I think we all have been through medical school at least once," she says, placing the vials on a small tray. "I'm going to run down the hall to the lab and make sure the blood is compatible for our purposes. Just sit tight."

"I'm not sure what to make of all this," Lauren says as Maria disappears out the door. She releases the cotton from her arm and reaches for his hand.

"I don't blame you," Dek replies. "We were paralyzed, kidnapped, brought to Charleston, introduced to a group who claims to be evolved, and now are linked to a firefight in the middle of downtown. And this is just today."

Glancing back at the doorway, Lauren whispers, "What do you think we should do? Maybe this is our chance to run?"

Dek thinks for a moment, then shakes his head. "I don't know. They seem to have a lot of answers for the questions we've been asking. I don't like the way they brought us here, but from the sound of that gunfight, it may have been just in the nick of time."

"You think that was someone looking for *us*?" Lauren asks, her brow furrowed in worry.

"I overheard Frenchy saying the Suburban was coming back with some of *our* things from the lake house," Dek says. "Maybe they thought you and I would be with our stuff? Either way, it may be safer for us to stay here, stay attentive, and see what we can learn."

Their attention is pulled to the hallway as they hear people thundering down the passage. Carson is pushing the heavily weighted gurney flanked by Philippe and a smaller Hispanic woman. The clothes of all three are splattered with blood. Decklan only glimpses the massive man lying on the gurney, his shoulder torn to pieces, as they rush past into the next room where Urvinder is suited up for surgery. Alexander and Thi Thi, their clothes rumpled but not bloodstained, follow the gurney at a brisk pace. They appear only mildly concerned as they approach Decklan and Lauren, who are standing in the doorway watching the commotion.

"I see that Maria went ahead and drew your blood as a precaution," Alexander says.

"Is he going to be okay?" asks Decklan, nodding his head toward the operating room.

"It will take more than a few gunshot wounds to take down that mountain of a man," Alexander says with a smile. "We'll patch him up and get him to the light room. An infusion of one of your blood samples should help to speed up the healing, and then we'll have our big man back in no time."

"What happened to them? Why were they attacked?" asks Lauren, inching past Dek.

"That is a long story, and it's late," Alexander says. "We'll go over everything in the morning when we all feel a little bit fresher." Alexander says a few quiet words to Thi Thi before he walks into the surgery room.

Thi Thi weaves them through a maze of corridors to a small elevator. They go up three floors and enter a dimly lit hallway. The old Victorian-style home has beautiful, richly stained baseboards, and thick crown moldings accentuate the tall ceilings. The hall is lined with heavily framed paintings; some are period pieces and some signed paintings are clearly from local artists.

Thi Thi stops at a large wooden door at the end of the hall. "This will be your room," she tells Dek, then adds somewhat clumsily, "Miss Lauren, will you be requiring your own room, or would you like to stay here?"

"Oh, er, this will be fine," Lauren replies with a sheepish grin.

"Alexander grabbed your bags from the truck before it was cleansed," Thi Thi informs them. "After we ensure there are no hidden trackers, I'll bring them up and place them outside the door."

"Our phones?" Lauren asks eagerly.

Thi Thi shrugs. "If they're in there, you'll have them." She clears her throat. "Out of an abundance of caution, though, please speak with us before you contact the outside world."

Dek glances at Lauren, and they slowly nod in agreement.

"If you need anything else, we can take care of it in the morning," Thi Thi says as she walks away.

Dek and Lauren stand at the door for a few seconds and watch her leave before entering the lavishly furnished bedroom.

"This room has got to be over six hundred square feet," says Decklan, admiring the twelve-foot ceilings with inset metallic tiles and intricately painted details.

"This must be one of the grand master bedrooms," Lauren says as she walks past the queen-size bed to an antique lounge chair positioned under a bank of windows. "All these windows will let in a ton of light in the morning," she points out. "I think we are on the southeastern corner .... I could use some sunlight."

Dek grins as he watches her walking around the room.

She feels the weight of his gaze and looks back at him, eyebrows pursed. "What are you smiling about?"

"I was just admiring the way you think. You were initially in awe, taking in the grandeur of our room. Then the science part of your brain can't help stepping in. *This is an east-facing window, the sun will be shining in each morning*," he says, mocking her playfully.

She tries to look annoyed, but she is delighted that he pays attention to even the smallest details of her personality. "Okay, goofy-dad-joke guy, you do realize that you already sound like an old man and you're not even thirty yet?" she retorts and sits on the edge of the bed.

"You like my humor ... I would describe it as not laugh-out-loud funny, but more smile-and-shake-your-head funny."

"Or just plain *not* funny," she says, smiling and shaking her head.

Decklan sits down next to her. "Hard to believe it's been less than twenty-four hours since all this began." He wraps his arm around her shoulders and gently pulls her in.

She rests her head on him. "I feel like our lives have been a crazy roller coaster since we met, and I don't see an end to the ride anywhere in sight .... Every laugh we can get is a welcome one."

"So you're saying, keep it up?" he says, lifting her chin and smiling down at her.

"Yep," she replies and moves into his kiss.

A short time later, they hear someone dropping their bags in the hallway.

"Do you think our phones will *really* be with the bags?" asks Lauren, hopping up from the bed.

"I mean, Thi Thi said they would be ...." Dek says, straightening his pants as he stands. "I'd be surprised, though, if they trust us with them."

Before he can catch up to her, Lauren peeks back in and lobs him a clear, ziplock bag holding both their phones. "That's a good sign."

Dek gently tosses the phones on the bed and hears Lauren grunt, struggling to lift their two bags at the same time.

"Hold up. I'm coming." Dek hauls their bags inside and shuts the door behind him. "I thought you had super strength?"

"Maybe I wanted to see if you were a true gentleman?" she replies, smiling. "You passed."

Lauren positions herself on the bed and extracts their phones, handing Dek his. "Okay, let's see what we've got going on," she says, curious to see if anyone noticed they were gone. "Grrrr. I hate this new fingerprint sensor ... wanna go back to using a PIN," she gripes under her breath. After realizing their old phones may have been tampered with, Dek and Lauren had to purchase new ones. Unfortunately, that shopping excursion occurred too late. Vincent had already tracked them and attacked them at the lake house that very night.

Dek smiles at her and patiently maneuvers his finger till his phone unlocks. He holds it up to listen to his voicemail. "Oh shit ... James is pissed .... Doesn't get why I hung up on him, then never called him back." He deletes one message, then listens to another. "Uh ... Houston ... we have a problem."

Lauren lowers her phone and eyes him wearily. "What now?"

"The guy who died at the lake house ... it was on the news, and James and Pam saw it. They've been trying to reach us ever since and apparently are heading down to see if we're okay."

"Shit," Lauren says, closing her eyes and pinching the bridge of her nose. "With all the violence that just went down near the Market, they could be heading into a dangerous situation."

"Do you think I should call him ... or ... I wonder if they'd"—he jerks his head toward the door—"be willing to send someone back to warn James off?" Dek looks down at his phone as if it holds the answer.

They sit in silence for a moment.

"I think," Lauren begins slowly, "our first step should be asking our hosts what they think ... how they think we should respond." Unease is written all over her face. "They did just save our lives, presumably ...."

Dek chews his lip. "Okay," he finally says and heads toward the door. "I'm going back downstairs to get some answers."

"I'm going too." Lauren jumps up and joins him.

They hurry downstairs and find Carson in the kitchen making a sandwich.

"Hey, Carson, we have a situation ...." Dek blurts out. "I just found out that my best friend and his fiancée are on their way to the lake house to check on us. Do you think they are in danger? How can we reach them to warn them?" His speech is so rushed, some of the words blend together.

Carson pauses with cheese in hand. He looks down at his sandwich and then emits a heavy sigh. He pulls out his phone. "Let me get Philippe, and we'll decide the best plan of action."

Once he dials, Carson immediately slaps the cheese and top piece of bread on his sandwich and takes a bite.

"Do you ever stop eating?" Dek asks.

"No!" Carson mumbles, attempting to chew and talk. "You know you want one now too."

Philippe answers dryly, "I think there is more mayonnaise in the pantry."

"Nah, man, I already found it .... I think we may have a problem, though. Can you come down to the kitchen?" he says, swallowing mid-sentence.

***

Philippe peers at them while shining an apple on his shirt. "When did you get the message?" he asks Dek.

"Uh ..." Dek flips through his phone for the call time and date. "Last night around four p.m."

"What *exactly* did they say?" Carson asks. "Let's hear it."

Dek sets his phone on the counter and plays the message on speaker.

What the shit, Dek! You ghost me for days? Richard's been killed, and now the news says someone died at your parents' lake house? I'm so pissed at you, but I'm worried, man .... I think ... yeah, Pam and I are coming down." The audio is garbled for a few seconds but they can hear a woman's voice in the background. *"We're leaving tonight. Should be down there Friday sometime around lunch. Meet us at the Wagon Wheel noon-ish, or I'm kicking your parents' front fuckin' door down.* Click.

"Well," Philippe says calmly, "the easiest way to fix this would be to call them and warn them off, but that may open us up to someone monitoring their phones to try to find out where you guys actually are .... The lake house is only about two hours away, right? We could try to intercept them tomorrow before they potentially put themselves at risk ...." He takes a bite of his apple and looks thoughtful. "It's going to be tricky if someone is watching the house—"

"We have to stop them at the restaurant," Carson interjects.

Philippe nods and brings up a map of the Fort Lawn area of South Carolina on his phone. He and Carson go back and forth arguing logistics.

Tapping her foot, Lauren asks, "It's already after midnight, do we leave now or go in the morning?"

Carson and Philippe shoot her questioning looks.

"Wait," Carson says with an incredulous shake of his head. "You two aren't going. You're staying here."

"Why wouldn't we go?" demands Lauren, her hands fisted at her hips. "Are we prisoners here or something?"

Philippe raises his hands in a calming motion. "No one is being held captive, but you just saw what people are willing to do to get a hold of you. It would be far safer for Carson and I to go."

"That would just raise more red flags for James," Dek warns. "He might even get the police involved."

Carson and Philippe exchange looks of frustration.

Eventually, Carson blows out a breath. "Okay, you can come with us," he concedes. "But if we say move, you move!"

"Grab whatever you need, and we'll head out in half an hour," Philippe says, alley-ooping the apple core into the trash can. "We can sleep in the van and scope out the area in the morning."

Thirty minutes later, they are on the road, going back to the lake house. As the excitement and adrenaline wear off, Dek and Lauren fall asleep. After two hours of no-traffic night driving, Carson pulls into a side street in a Fort Lawn neighborhood near the house. He throws the car in park and lets out a tired sigh. He lowers the volume on the radio and tilts his head back for a brief rest. Whether it's the lack of motion or noise from the front seat, something wakes Dek and Lauren. Philippe stretches his seat belt and turns around, chuckling as they gawk at his transformation.

"Well, that's a look," says Lauren, rubbing her eyes as she takes in his bushy hair and full beard.

"We are only a few blocks from the house. I'm going to go and do some recon," says Philippe, quietly opening the door. "I'll be back in an hour."

After a quick update on the general plan, Dek and Lauren snuggle together in the back seat of the van, now too wide awake to sleep again.

A slight rustling of leaves is the only warning they have before Philippe returns with a silent opening of the passenger door. "There isn't anyone at the house, but two men are sitting in a car just off the road on the only vehicle route to the house."

"Did you get a good look at them?" Carson asks.

Philippe nods. "One is on his phone watching a video; the other is asleep. They are not from the same group that attacked us by the Market, but I think we need to presume they also have some military training."

"We could take them out and then meet your friends less publicly, at the house," Carson suggests. Looking around at three skeptical faces, he sighs. "Or we could go with the original plan and meet at the restaurant, sending your friends home before they get into trouble."

"With two men watching the house, I like the OG plan a lot better," confirms Dek, shaking his head at the prospect of "taking someone out."

Philippe confirms the plan of action. "Okay, let's all get some rest," he says. "We'll take you to the restaurant tomorrow, then Carson will go back and watch the men at the lake to make sure you have uninterrupted time."

At eleven a.m. the Wagon Wheel opens, and Dek and Lauren are among the first to be seated. They request a table with a good view of the entrance and surreptitiously nod a few minutes later when Philippe comes in as a solo and sits at the counter. After half an hour of fried squash and hush puppy appetizers, Dek notices a clearly agitated Philippe talking on his phone. He watches Philippe get up from his seat, put a handful of cash on the counter, and stalk over to them.

"What's up?" asks Dek, glancing around for a sign of danger.

"The men watching the house are on the move. Carson thinks they may be coming here for lunch," Philippe says.

"The house is just a few minutes from here," Lauren says nervously.

"We need to get out of here now," Philippe replies quietly, setting some money down on their table. "I'll check it out first; you two wait by the bathrooms in the lobby."

Philippe looks out the front door into the parking lot, then quickly walks across the lobby to Dek and Lauren. "Shit, this may be where they are doing a surveillance shift switch. Two new guys of similar look and vehicle are walking this way now," he says, pushing Dek and Lauren toward the bathrooms. "Hide in the stalls! I'll get you when it's clear."

Philippe feigns interest in the ad board in the lobby as the two men walk in from the parking lot. He overhears them as they greet the hostess, saying they are meeting two friends. The hostess grabs four menus and shows them to their table.

When they leave the room, Philippe darts to the bathrooms, rapping on the doors. "Quick, quick," he urges, as Dek and Lauren peek out. "Go along the building toward the back," he whispers, shooing them out.

Lauren power walks out first, followed by Dek, who is literally shoved out by Philippe quickly shutting the door behind him when one of the men returns to the lobby.

"Get me a root beer. I just gotta wash my hands," the guy calls out to his friend. He gives Philippe a questioning look before entering the bathroom.

Outside, Lauren glances back as Dek crashes into her from Philippe's shove. Dek quickly grabs her hand and they scurry around toward the back of the restaurant. The car with the two men from the lake pulls in just as they round the corner. Dek takes a quick glance back, looking for Philippe. He whips his head back around the corner when two military-looking men get out of the sedan and head inside.

"This is a mistake. I think we need to get out of here," Lauren whispers, casting glances all around them.

The gods couldn't have timed it better. As soon as the restaurant's front door closes, they hear James yell across the lot.

"Decklan Thomas, you dick! You're lucky you're here!"

Dek and Lauren push off the wall, smiling nervously. They quickly walk toward James's car as he climbs out of the driver's side.

"How are you, buddy?" Dek asks in a half whisper. "Listen, I can explain everything, but not here .... They're, uh, doing a private lunch today and, um, closed to the general public. Bummer, huh?" Dek jabbers on, rapid fire, as he guides James back into the car. He closes the driver's door, then bends and sticks his head inside the open window. "Hey, Pam! So there is another place a couple of blocks down called Gene's. Let's go there .... Mind if Lauren and I ride with you? We can easily walk back for our car." Dek opens the back door for Lauren and they hop in. "Gosh, it's so good to see you guys."

James gives Pam a questioning look, then shrugs his shoulders. "I mean, we came here to see you guys ... so, sure, let's go."

Lauren lightly elbows Dek and nods out the window. They watch Carson's van slow down to pick up Philippe, then follow behind them.

The van sits idly outside Gene's parking lot while the foursome enters the restaurant.

After they order, Dek spends many long minutes apologizing and groveling. Lauren interjects when she can to reinforce his much-censored story.

"No, no. He didn't hang up on you; his phone fell in the water ...."

"I'm sorry, man, I don't know your damn number off the top of my head ...."

"We were just enjoying some quiet time after the craziness with Richard ...."

Finally, James punches Dek in the arm—hard—and seems to accept Dek and Lauren's version of events. As the food arrives, a much more relaxed James and Pam share some stories that border on slapstick about how frantic they had been to get down there.

Dek shakes with laughter. "I appreciate your concern, guys!"

"You two should try and enjoy a few relaxing days in Charlotte before going home," Lauren tells them.

Dek and Lauren offer them suggestions for things they could do, and soon enough, James and Pam are heading back to Charlotte and Dek and Lauren are getting in the van.

"Are we good?" asks Philippe, looking back at them in the passenger side mirror.

Dek and Lauren both nod. Lauren rests her head on Dek's shoulder. "We're good," she confirms.

"It was so nice to just meet friends and enjoy a double date, small talk, old times, and jokes," she comments, closing her eyes.

"Yeah, life almost seemed normal for a minute there." Dek glances down at her. "I knew you liked my jokes."

They ride back to Charleston in relative silence.

CHAPTER 5

The next day, when the heat of the morning sun spreads across their bed through the eastern-facing window, Lauren is the first to open her eyes. She peers around, taking in the entirety of their room in the daylight. She eases closer to Decklan and runs her hand over his bare chest to gently wake him up. He stretches his back and turns, wrapping her in his arms.

"I know it's strange, given the circumstances, but there is just something about this place. I feel like we're on vacation," she whispers, kissing his chest before relaxing her head against him.

Dek kisses the top of her head and lazily gazes out the window. "I know what you mean, after the excitement of yesterday. I feel like we can decompress now … *and* get some answers."

They lay there for a few more minutes, soaking in the peace. "I would guess it's about seven o'clock," Lauren says through a yawn. "Go back to sleep or get up?"

He groans softly, putting his free hand on his forehead. "I am so glad to have some peace of mind with regard to James, but we should probably get up."

They languidly roll out of bed and after a quick change, ride the elevator down to the main floor and find the kitchen.

The kitchen opens up to a large veranda stretching along the entire back of the house. The veranda leads into a grand courtyard connecting all of the houses on the square block. Each surrounding house has a veranda and three tiers of balconies looking onto the courtyard's garden. Large wrought iron fences built between the houses protect the garden from passersby, and the dense growth of the garden blocks any view of the courtyard from the street. Dek and Lauren walk onto the veranda and into the middle of a spirited conversation.

"I can't believe it," Maria says. "The Evos have never made a move like this before. It threatens to expose us all! Has Ra lost his mind?"

"That's exactly what I thought, but when I saw Anubis I just knew something was going down," replies the woman they saw in the corridor the night before. Both women are dressed in workout tanks and leggings.

Frenchy jumps up from his seat when he sees the couple. "Ahh, my friends, good morning. I hope you slept well. Would you like something to eat? Coffee, tea?"

"Coffee would be great. Thanks, Frenchy," says Lauren.

He starts for the door then stops. "Oh, pardon my manners. This is Cleo; she came in late last night—you may have seen her in passing. Please grab a seat, I'll be right back." He pulls out a chair for Lauren before retreating to the kitchen.

"Hi, Cleo. I'm Lauren and this is Decklan. Thank you for getting some of our things for us. I'm so sorry about your friend; will he be okay?" asks Lauren, taking the seat next to Cleo.

"I don't know if you saw him? He's a pretty big guy, makes for an easy target. He's been shot before and probably will be shot again .... If you had stayed at the lake house, we would've been the ones to pick you up. You were much better off with Urvinder's soft touch," she says with a smile.

"When we walked out here, you were talking about the Evos and Ra. Is that who attacked you last night?" asks Decklan, carefully prying for some answers.

Cleo looks over to Maria. "He didn't give them his full intro speech?" she asks.

"You guys cut him off before he could get to the good stuff."

Cleo clears her throat. "I'm not sure Alexander wants me to be the one to talk to you about—"

"Did I hear someone mentioning my name?" asks Alexander as he and Thi Thi come walking across the garden on a quaint stone pathway that snakes through the flowers, bisecting the courtyard.

A chorus of good mornings erupts from the table.

"Yes, good morning," echoes Frenchy, returning from the kitchen. He sets down a tray containing a coffeepot, cups, and a plate of pastries. "Just in time for some breakfast. Is there anything you two would like? I brought out some pastries, because I know this crew is always hungry."

"We had a bite just now before coming over," says Alexander, stopping about three feet from the table. "We are going to check on our injured friend." He turns toward Dek and Lauren and adds, "Let's plan on finishing our talk this afternoon." Without waiting for their response, Alexander begins to usher Thi Thi away.

Cleo shoves her chair back and stands. "Wait. I'll go with you guys. I've barely left his side since we got here, but I'm due to annoy him." She grins at Dek and Lauren. "Nice to meet you two. I'm sure we'll talk later."

The veranda grows quiet.

Decklan and Lauren sip their coffee. Maria chooses a pastry and begins nibbling.

"Are you coming from or going to a workout?" Lauren asks, breaking the awkward silence. "I would love to get the blood flowing."

Maria holds a finger up. "Going," she says after swallowing her bite. "I'm planning to work out with Carson. Would you both like to come?"

Lauren turns to Dek and raises an eyebrow.

He shrugs. "Sounds good. I'm way overdue to work out."

"Great. When you finish eating, get changed and meet us in the center gym." Maria points to a large main-floor room in the western corner of the house they are sitting behind. She dabs her mouth with a napkin, then gets up from the table. "I'm eager to see what you got," she quips.

* * *

"You look ready to pump some iron," Frenchy awkwardly jokes when he runs into Decklan and Lauren at the foot of the stairs. He motions down the hallway. "The gym is just down there to the left." He waits until the two enter the room, then turns and walks down the opposite hallway to a darkened staircase descending into the basement.

The lower hallway is a dimly lit tunnel lined with doorways. About halfway is a room ablaze with fluorescent lights. Frenchy enters the glowing doorway into the sunroom. The room is large, about thirty by thirty, and looks a lot like an emergency room. There are three beds lining the wall, separated by curtains, each with their own sets of health-monitoring equipment. To the left of the door on the far wall is one large bed, containing one giant man, lined by an array of bright lights simulating intense sunlight.

His eyes quickly adjusting to the bright lights, Frenchy crosses the room to stand next to Alexander, Urvinder, and Thi Thi, who are just outside of the lights' glow. Cleo is seated on the far side of the bed, shadowed by Brutus, who is sitting up in the inclined bed with his left shoulder heavily bandaged.

"It looks like our patient is feeling better," Frenchy says.

"I'm a little rough, but I think I'll pull through," replies Brutus, his deep voice echoing off the basement walls.

"The attack on Brutus and Cleo was clearly meant to take our new guests from our care—a bold move, even for Ra," Alexander says, rubbing his chin pensively with his left hand.

"Sending his top people and having a firefight in downtown Charleston ..." Cleo pauses. "He must think Decklan and Lauren know where the virus came from. Clearly, he is ready to release the virus on the world and damn the consequences."

"He has been ready to do that for some time," Alexander says grimly. "The fact that these two encountered the virus in a northern

US city as well as his belief in the timeline of pi … he is using this as justification for causing the release of the ninth evolutionary virus, and the next major evolutionary jump."

"If he's so determined to get them, what's to stop him from attacking us here?" asks Frenchy in an anxious tone.

"We have a nonviolence pact with regard to this sanctum," Alexander says, patting Frenchy's shoulder reassuringly. "I think that's the reason he attacked them outside of the Market. Besides, Maria has this place fully secured. The more important question is, if Ra is able to determine that the virus that changed Decklan and Lauren originated from a viable site, to what extent is he willing to move forward with his plans?"

CHAPTER 6

A truck full of supplies jumps and jostles its way along the potholed dirt road that leads to the Helms Chemical mining camp in Ecuador. Rounding one more corner, the driver sees the makeshift gate and guard station come into view. The truck is quickly waved along by the two guards, who slide open the gate.

The truck continues into the jungle clearing that is home to the small camp. There is a fifty-yard straight path culminating in a larger command hut. Parked dump trucks, large cranes, and industrial mining excavators line either side of the main road. The height of the vehicles gives the impression of driving through a gorge. The truck comes to a stop at the end of the path in front of the command hut, and the driver cuts off the engine and prepares his delivery paperwork. He can hear the sounds of heavy machinery drowning out the normally serene sounds of the jungle. Then there's a sudden explosion followed by the crashing and grinding of metals and, finally, shouts of agony.

Captain Santiago, the camp leader, lunges through the mosquito netting door at the back of the main camp office to see a large cloud of smoke rising above the trees in the direction of the primary dig site. "Shit! What the hell now!" he yells, tearing the sweat-soaked hat from his head and slamming it on the decking. A safety truck and hose crew speed by, heading to the fire. A man covered in dirt and soot staggers out of the jungle and falls to the ground, gasping for air.

The captain jumps over the handrailing and runs to the fallen man. "José! José," he yells as he kneels next to him. "Are you okay?"

Coughing, the man looks up, his eyes blood red from the smoke and ash. "Pickup truck ... rammed our main drilling rig ...." He pants, struggling to regain his breath. "Must have been filled with fuel ... or explosives ...."

Another safety truck pulls around the office, and three more men come dashing out the back door. A fourth man, tall and thin, follows. He looks up at the billows of smoke snaking skyward over the trees and rests his hands heavily on the railing, slowly shaking his head.

"You men!" yells Captain Santiago, still crouching next to the coughing man. "Tend to José." He jumps up, waving down the safety truck. "I'll go to the drill site and check on the damage." The truck slows, allowing him to jump on the side rail. He gives a frustrated grimace to the tall man on the deck as he signals the driver to continue on.

The tall man holds open the door as José is brought into a small infirmary located to the right of the command hut. "Gracias, Feldman," says one of the men attempting to get José comfortable.

One man runs to a cabinet to grab the portable oxygen. Another man grabs some supplies and begins to clean José's wounds. After several minutes of deep breaths, José starts talking again. Feldman stands quietly at the back of the room, listening as he recites the events leading up to the explosion.

"I had just gone to take a piss and was walking back when the truck cleared the jungle wall," José says between hits of oxygen. "The crash was one thing, but the explosion that followed was something else. We must have had ten or more men working the rig when it happened ...."

Feldman nods his head to one of the men before disappearing into one of the smaller side offices. He picks up his phone, pausing for a second to collect his thoughts before hitting the speed dial marked with an *H*.

"This had better be a report of good news and progress?" Mr. Helms says when he answers.

"Not quite, sir," Feldman responds apologetically. "We've had another accident at the drill site. As far as I can tell, a man drove a pickup filled with explosives into our main rig. The equipment is damaged, and there will definitely be casualties."

"Shit! Do we know who was behind the attack?"

Feldman begins pacing the small room. "It's early, but based on some of the other trouble we've been having, we think it's the locals." He scoffs. "They have a hardened belief that this land holds some kind of demon or plague, and that our mining project will release it."

"You have got to be fucking kidding me?" Helms says, frustration causing his voice to crack. "This bullshit again? One of our guides died of cancer down there ... what, five years ago? Why that drew every superstitious wacko out of the woodwork is beyond me." He sighs heavily. "Listen, we have a ton of money invested in this—"

"I know. I'm working on it," Feldman interjects. "I have a guy trying to identify the, er, troublemakers." He shakes his head. "You wouldn't believe some of the shit I've heard, sir. The communities here are very spiritual and apparently refer back to an ancient writing that claimed death would come to those who disturbed the land."

Helms snorts. "We did our best to dispel those rumors years ago when we were first down there doing the prelim soil tests .... Some people will only believe what they want to believe. But, Feldman, we cannot allow this project to be sabotaged by nutjobs."

"Yes, sir. I'll have the cleanup crew assess the site and see if we can proceed with the dig—"

"We will proceed with the dig," Helms says frostily. "I'm not letting some crazy fuckers put a stop to my plans. We will extract the metal!" He pauses to regain his composure but his tone remains cool. "I'll be heading back down soon. In the meantime, I'll contact some military contractors to help investigate and provide a safe working environment at the site. Feldman, are we clear?"

"Yes, sir. I'll work from my end and you can work from yours," Feldman murmurs, hastily adding, "I look forward to seeing you when you arrive."

Helms throws his phone on his desk and walks over to the window. Drawing a few deep breaths and some strength from the New York City skyline, he turns to a dark cabinet in the corner. He places his thumb over the scanner, and the wooden panel slides down. A soft purple light illuminates a small filter suspended between cables within the enclosure. He stares at it and thinks, *So many problems, but in the end, it will all be worth it.*

CHAPTER 7

Through a pair of floor-to-ceiling windows on either side of the gym door, Dek and Lauren can see Carson and Maria stretching. They enter after Dek knocks softly.

"Hey guys, got room for two more?" he says as his gaze scopes out the equipment.

The large, rectangular room has banks of mirrors spaced out along the walls, enabling views from almost every angle. Two squat racks and two bench press areas are situated along the outer wall, a large cable machine sits in the middle, and a free weights area is on the inner wall. The corner near where they entered has floor mats for stretching or yoga, which is where Carson and Maria are. Dek and Lauren walk over and join them.

"You both look like you're in pretty good shape," says Maria, leaning over her outstretched leg as she sizes up the new arrivals.

"Dek works out a little more regularly than I do," says Lauren. "But I managed to hold my own when we exercised in Chicago."

"You definitely did," Dek says, eyeing her ass as she stretches. "And looked damn delicious doing it," he adds with an exaggerated wink at Carson. A beat of silence follows, then Dek sees Carson and Maria exchange knowing glances. "That was just a little joke," Dek mutters uncomfortably.

Maria turns toward Lauren. "You know this is a Newbie thing?" she says, nodding at Dek. "When a man is first evolved, his hormones are amped up, like he's a teenager times ten."

Carson laughs at Dek's mortified expression. "Man, you're receiving so many new visual and hormonal signals that you couldn't sense before, and at a rapid-fire pace. A week after I first changed, I went out to the club with Philippe. Not a good idea. That is already a high-stimulation arena. My inappropriate comments almost got me slapped at least a half-dozen times."

Shaking her head at Dek as if he were a mischievous child, Maria adds, "As annoying as it is, it's fairly common to hear Newbie men carelessly spouting inappropriate comments due to how strongly those signals are coming in."

"With time and a little training," Carson says, getting up from the mat, "you'll learn how to filter and control your responses." He pats Dek on the shoulder as he passes him. "First lesson, you don't have to say everything that pops into your head."

"Yes, sensei," Dek says, placing his hands together and bowing slightly. "Please help me stop putting my foot in my mouth."

Moments later, Carson breaks up their laughter. "All right, get your asses up," he says. "Time to train."

Dek works out with Carson, focusing more on lifting heavy weights, way more than Dek could ever dream he could lift.

"You are doing really well," says Carson, spotting Dek at the bench press. "Your muscles will respond naturally to handle the stress that you put them under, increasing muscle fibers and elasticity, and strengthening your tendons and ligaments to handle the load."

They rack the weight. "Wow, I feel great," Dek says, breathing heavily after his set. "My buddy James and I would work out on a regular schedule when I was at Madison, but never using this kind of poundage."

Carson starts loading another two plates on each side of the bar and clamps it into place.

"You are really going to show me up here, loading up the bar like that?" Dek asks, looking at the impressive weight on the bar.

"Oh no," says Carson, sliding back into his spotting position. "This is for you, big guy. Focus and ask your muscles to do more."

"You're kidding," Dek says, shifting around and noticing that the women are coming over to see if he can do it. "I have never attempted even one hundred pounds close to this weight."

Carson leans over and gently grabs Dek by the shoulders. "You got this, man," he says with an encouraging shake.

Dek shoots Lauren a worried glance and lies back down on the bench, taking a few deep breaths and finding his hand placement on the bar.

"Now concentrate, Dek," says Maria, standing next to Lauren. "Focus on your muscles. Make them do the work."

Dek gets the bar up with a liftoff from Carson. The bar goes down but doesn't move an inch back up. "UGH!" Dek gasps. "Can't do it."

Carson yanks the bar back to its stand.

Lauren gives him a hand, up to a sitting position. "I give you credit for even trying."

"You can handle that weight," says Carson, walking around and removing the weights from the bar. "You just have to get past the mental roadblocks that are still holding you back. The only barriers evolved humans have are the ones we place on ourselves. The best advice I can give you moving forward is work on meditation. Learn how to communicate with your cells, and they will not fail you."

Dek and Lauren finish the workout using more weight than they ever have before but not taking it to the level that Dek tried at the weight bench. After a quick cooldown stretch, Maria and Carson head back to their rooms, leaving Dek and Lauren alone on the mats.

"Well, that felt great," Lauren says. "I haven't worked out like that ... well, I've never worked out like that before." She shakes her head in disbelief. "I can really feel the strong connection between mind and body when concentrating only on exercising, rather than constantly using my muscles to save myself from, like, a deadly situation. The difference between the body acting reflexively, versus consciously asking the body to respond, really demonstrates how much potential there is in the human body."

"Carson said that I should work on meditation to help connect with my cells on a deeper level," Dek says, then glances toward the door. "Hey, do you think he and Maria are a couple?"

She shrugs. "Not sure. They may have had a different relationship at one time, but I would say just friends." She gets to her feet. "It's strange to think about—they both look like they're in their thirties, but they could be in their seventies for all we know."

"So much about our lives is strange," Dek says with a laugh. "I cannot believe we are sitting here, casually discussing the possibility of our *captors* having a relationship."

Lauren smiles. "Yup, that's really weird." She heaves him to his feet.

As he rises up to her eye level, he notices that she is smiling at him in a thoughtful way.

"What is that look?" he asks, smiling back at her.

"Oh nothing, I was just thinking that you look good. That's all," she says, turning toward the door with a swoosh of her hair.

"Well, that's the best thing I've heard all day." He replies, hurrying after her.

"So are you up for a shower?" she asks with an exaggerated eyebrow waggle.

Dek looks down at her. "As in *together*, hot stuff?" he asks with a grin. "Shoot .... Inappropriate ... sorry!"

Lauren laughs. "Look, they may have a point about talking so overtly in public, but you can keep gushing over me in private all you want!"

CHAPTER 8

A sharp knock at the door interrupts Dek and Lauren from their afternoon nap.

"At your convenience, please join Alexander on the rooftop terrace for afternoon cocktails," Frenchy relays to them through the door.

"Sounds great, Frenchy. Just give us a few minutes to freshen up," replies Lauren, excited at the prospect of some new information.

Dek lets out a slight yawn. "We definitely have to have 'quality time' more often," he says with a devilish grin.

"I think I need another shower before I can hang out with evolved people," Lauren says, jumping out of bed and hurrying into the bathroom, still naked. "This heightened-sense-of-smell thing has me feeling self-conscious."

They both end up showering again, this time separately. They meet Frenchy as he is coming up the main staircase with a large tray of meats, cheeses, and chopped-up fruits and vegetables. "This way," he says, nodding down the hallway to a large spiral staircase curving up to an open doorway.

"I could really smell the ocean air in the hall," Dek says as they climb the stairs. "I thought someone had the windows open."

They come out to a twenty-by-twenty veranda lined with beautiful plants in an array of colorful pots and planters. They take in the expansive view of the harbor from the railing, watching boats drift in and out and soaking up the strong afternoon sunrays.

"This is quite a view you have here," Lauren says a few moments later as they stroll over to Alexander and Thi Thi.

"Please, come enjoy the summer afternoon with us," Alexander says, motioning them to sit in the empty swivel sling chairs around a table adorned with expensive-looking china and silverware.

Frenchy sets down the food in the middle of the table and walks over to a small console tucked away among the plants. He sets up a bucketful of ice and brings it to them with a chilled bottle of wine and four wineglasses. "Such a beautiful day. It would be a waste to just spend it inside."

"I know you both must be hungry after getting in *such* a workout today," says Alexander with a knowing grin. "Let's not let any of this wonderful food go to waste. Please dig in."

The sun is kicking his cells into overdrive, and Dek realizes he is starving. He quickly makes a small pile of sandwiches and then notices Lauren grimacing at his lack of manners.

"I'm so sorry," he says to Alexander, looking for a way to return some of the food.

"No, no, it's perfectly fine. We have all gone through it," says Alexander, glancing at Thi Thi.

She nods. "In the first year or so after the evolution, you will still have some active virus floating around in your system," Thi Thi says. "This will become more active in the presence of sunlight. Bringing you out here in front of a large tray of food is almost unfair."

"She is right," Alexander says with a smile. "Let's enjoy our food, then I'll be happy to answer some of your questions."

Dek tries his best to dine politely but still eats multiple plates of food in seemingly record time.

"You will find that eating more plant-based food or calorie-dense food will sate you better than processed foods," says Thi Thi after finishing her much-smaller plate of food. "Your new digestive cells will be able to handle all of the preservatives and other processed chemicals, but you will truly be able to feel how much better for you it is to eat a more natural diet."

Sitting back from the table and dabbing the corners of her mouth with a napkin, Lauren gives Alexander a let's-get-down-to-business look. "So what else can you tell us?" she asks rather bluntly.

Dek, who is swallowing his latest bite, quickly looks up from his food and chuckles at her take-no-prisoners posture.

If Alexander is offended by Lauren's directness, he does not let on. "It seems like every time that I have this conversation with a newly evolved person," he begins, "it changes and modernizes based on the new information that we are constantly learning about this amazing process." Alexander picks up his wineglass and takes a small sip. "Let me begin with the full account of my personal experience, and I'll tell you what I've learned up until today.

"I was born in 1884 in a small village outside of Moscow, and though we were farmers, I was fortunate to attend university. I specialized in archaeology and traveled with a group to Central Africa. We visited some of the ancient sites and were permitted to inspect the active diamond and mineral mines nearby. One night, my friend Victor asked if I wanted to visit an abandoned mine that would likely have an abundance of gems. We went just after nightfall in a group of four: Victor and I and two men who would act as our guides. Along the way, our guides told us the lore of the 'cursed' mine, that it was abandoned quickly after a plague caused many of the workers to die. At this time in Africa, mining was a booming business with lots of competition. It was not unusual for mining companies to hide valuable mines behind stories of cursed or poisoned workers, just to keep thieves away."

Alexander pauses and gently swirls his glass of wine. He notices Lauren squirm, eager for him to continue, and smiles at her. "We did indeed find a bounty of ore and minerals and returned to the camp with as many samples as we could carry. The next morning, Victor and I met with the other two men and tore through our samples with mallet and brush to isolate what we deemed valuable. I still remember the morning sun was particularly strong that day, and we were dusty and sweaty when we said our goodbyes and went to pack up. But Victor and I never made it to our tents .... When I woke, I had the distinct memory of people yelling and screaming. It was late in the afternoon and the camp was torn up. Victor was beside me on the ground, but everyone else was gone. Fortunately, I was able to rouse him and we walked around trying to determine what hap—"

"Please don't tell me everyone in the camp died?" asks Lauren, fearing the virus might be a lot more deadly than they initially thought.

"No," replies Alexander. "We found our two guides dead, and one woman whose tent was near where we cleaned our samples had also died. We believe panic spread and caused everyone else to flee. Victor and I spent the next two days waiting for the disease to take us, but we noticed that we actually felt better, not worse. In fact, we felt *a lot* better than we had ever felt before, so we packed up our supplies and made our way to Cairo, where we sold some of the diamonds and gems that we mined. That first sale was so successful, that within a ridiculously short period of time, we had an import-export company without rival.

"It was obvious to us that we now had quite an advantage over our fellow man. Physically, we were indeed superior—we *never* suffered from illness—and we continually realized new abilities. One day I noticed I had a photographic memory; the next day, the uncanny ability to determine when people were lying. It really wasn't fair—"

"We also have the ability to detect lies!" Dek blurts out. "I mean, we're able to pick up on the physical signs of lying: pupil dilation and heartbeat change—"

Lauren elbows him lightly. "He knows, Dek," she tells him with a laugh. "So how many others like you did you find during this time?" she asks Alexander. "Were their abilities similar?"

"Actually, we did not find anyone for many years," Alexander responds matter-of-factly. "But to be fair, we didn't exactly know what to look for, and we were focused on enjoying the life we had built. The news of a growing economy drew us to America, just near the beginning of the Roaring Twenties. We initially settled here in Charleston since its harbor gave us a new port of access; at that point, we were exporting gems and minerals from Africa to countries throughout all of Europe and Asia." He drums his fingers on the table. "It wasn't until the summer of 1930 that we met another."

Alexander smiles at the memory. "We were holding a fundraiser to help those caught in the ravages of the Depression, when it seemed as if the people parted and a tiny, five-foot-one wisp of a woman, who just exuded confidence, stopped in front of us. She looked us over, then a hum started to fill our ears, soft at first but soon sounding like a train. Victor and I were well able to quiet our cells when need be, but we both had to cover our ears." He turns to Dek and says sheepishly, "We must have looked quite silly as we were the only three who could hear this sound."

Alexander thrust his hands out front theatrically. "'Okay, okay!' I told the lady, prompting her to turn down the volume. The three of us retired to the study and exchanged our tales, or shall I say Victor and I told her our tale; Urvinder barely told us any of her story. I still, to this day, do not know much more about that woman than she was educated as a physician."

Hoping he wouldn't be considered terribly rude, Dek took the opportunity to ask one of his biggest questions. "How does she do that little trick of hers, making people freeze?"

"No clue," Alexander says simply. "She showed us that ability sometime in the seventies, taking us all by surprise. I know that Frenchy, for one, has tried for many years to figure it out."

Dek turns to find the man standing at the railing watching the boats. "Any luck, Frenchy?"

"Damned if I know," he says without turning around.

Lauren and Thi Thi laugh.

"Where is Victor now?" Lauren asks. "It sounds like you were very close."

"We had a little falling-out over a disagreement in philosophy, and he left us," Alexander says coolly. "By that time, we had found many others who had evolved, including our friend over there." He nodded to Frenchy. "He had been working in an upscale hotel in Morocco, leading the service staff and maybe picking a pocket or two."

Frenchy breezes over to them. "I feel that I was saved and whisked away to the States to my true calling: master of the library," he says, swishing his arm playfully.

They chuckle, and Frenchy begins to collect the tray and remnants of food. "Does anyone need anything else?" he asks from the doorway.

"I think we're all good," says Alexander, standing up. "I think it's time for me to take a little nap. You know, I'm not one hundred and ten anymore."

Thi Thi and Alexander walk together to the stairs and leave Dek and Lauren alone on the terrace.

"Wow, that was a crazy story," Dek says. He reaches for Lauren and tugs her to her feet. He rubs his thumb lightly on the back of her hand as they amble over to the railing.

She nods in agreement, eyes on the boats below.

He twirls her into his chest, hugging her from behind, and speaks softly in her ear. "I didn't pick up any signs that he wasn't telling us the truth. Did you?"

"Well," Lauren begins carefully, "we can tell if regular people are lying. Can we—who evolved mere weeks ago—tell if someone who evolved hundreds of years ago is lying?" She shrugs. "I'm not sure we can, unless he wanted us to …."

"I suppose you have a point there," Dek says quietly. "Did you find it strange how Frenchy distanced himself from being directly involved in the story, and yet hung around close enough to listen?"

Lauren strains her neck to look at him. She shakes her head. "I didn't notice at the time," she says. "But you're right. I'm not sure what that could mean, though."

Dek blows out a breath. "Well, let's just continue to be careful here. Maybe I'm just paranoid from our time in Chicago," he says, referring to the recording devices found in their hotel room, "but I keep getting the feeling that we're being watched and listened to all the time."

She frowns. "It would be nice to have a night away from here and get some privacy," she says before leaning in for a kiss.

CHAPTER 9

An all-black Dodge Charger with oversize shiny silver rims turns down a roughly paved driveway located just outside of North Charleston. The driveway slices through about two acres of heavily forested land, culminating at a large metal gate guarding the opening of an ivy-covered brick fence. Buttressed by two hulking stone pillars topped with grotesquely carved gargoyles, the gate automatically slides open as the car approaches. The smooth drive leads up to a towering old Southern plantation-style mansion. The gated yard is well-kept, with outcroppings of azaleas and roses highlighting some intricately carved statues of men's and women's bodies topped with the heads of animals, more reminiscent of ancient Egypt than the American South.

The car stops at the top of the circular drive just outside the steps leading up to the wraparound front porch. A tall, thin man wearing a tan summer suit gets out of the Charger and enters through the stately front door. He walks through an ornately decorated foyer into a large, open room lined with paintings and wall hangings matching the Southern style of the house. Four men playing cards around a square dining table look up, taking notice of the man briefly before returning to their game. He turns and exits the room through an arched door on the left wall and traverses a short hallway to a set of double glass doors.

The heat and humidity hit him immediately as he enters the enormous glass-walled greenhouse, weaving his way along a stone path lined with a beautiful variety of flowers and plants, finally coming to a fountain with a surrounding five-foot pool. Two women are sitting at a small patio table having drinks.

A man wearing tan shorts and a white button-down shirt is spritzing water on some bright-yellow flowers just on the other side of the fountain. "You're late," he says calmly, his gaze remaining focused on his task.

The tall man nods to the women sitting at the table before responding. "Traffic," he says simply.

The man continues to spray the flowers. "What do you think, Isis? Was Anubis stuck in traffic or just taking his own sweet time, as he usually does?"

The woman closer to Anubis swipes her black curls out of her face to get a better look at him. "Maybe," she replies, adjusting her flowy skirt around her crisscross legs. "But I've definitely heard that one from him before."

"And you, Osiris, with your keen eye for detail, what do you think?" he asks the other woman.

Osiris's dress is more businesslike and her long blond hair is in a slick ponytail. She looks up from her book and gives Anubis a knowing once-over. "Hmm, judging by the blade of grass stuck in his shoe and the hint of sweat around his sunglasses ... driving range?"

Anubis laughs. "I may have hit a few balls this morning," he says, his Australian accent easily perceptible. "But I also was stuck in traffic, love." He makes a noisy production of dragging out the chair next to Isis and reversing it so he can sit backward. "I would never keep Ra waiting intentionally. It's hard enough as it is pulling him away from his beautiful plants."

Ra, cringing as he hears the heavy chair scraping the ground, finally turns his gaze on his guests. "You will soon learn the global importance of my beautiful plants," he says, waving his arm to draw their eyes to the large trees lining the side of the greenhouse. "Enough with the small talk. What have you to report?"

Osiris snaps her book closed and launches into her account before Anubis can get a word out. "As far as we can tell, there is no blowback from our failed attempt to capture the two new Evos. Apparently, they were in a different car," she says dryly. "They are now heavily guarded within the compound. Our intel inside indicates that they are fully evolved and would be good blood donors if we need to create more Newbies. As to how they evolved, it seems to be associated with a lab accident, but there's been some sort of cover-up. If I can find out who covered it up, we can discover where the virus originated."

"Does *Alexander* know the source of their viral encounter?" Ra asks as he walks closer to them.

Osiris thrums her fingers on the cover of her hardback. "The information that I'm getting suggests that the pair haven't said, and Alexander isn't probing them for information."

Ra drops the spritzer on the table and takes a seat. "Do we think Alexander is purposely not asking them because he suspects one of his people will leak the information to us?" he asks casually.

"I have no indication that our source is compromised, but I can ask them to lay even lower," Osiris replies. "They already know it's too valuable to risk reporting on the day-to-day."

"The evolution of these two is the sign we've been waiting for," Ra says. "The virus is fighting to find a way out, to change the world, and bring on the ninth evolution." He slaps his knee in excitement. "We must find out!"

"If they know the origin of the virus that infected them, we'll get the information from them," Osiris says.

"That's wonderful, love, but if we'd have gotten them at the Market, we'd be on the move for the virus right now," Anubis says, clearly frustrated that his ambush didn't bear fruit despite his brilliant planning.

"Yes, but we totally took them by surprise," Isis reassures him. "I haven't been able to let loose like that in years."

Anubis takes Isis's hand. "It was truly beautiful, seeing my warrior woman flying down those stairs guns a-blazing. It takes me back to when we first met ....” he says, his voice trailing off dramatically.

Ra exchanges here-we-go-again looks with a clearly tired-of-hearing-the-story Osiris. “Back to the point ...” she says, trying to interject, but Isis jumps to her feet, cradling Anubis's hand in hers as she tugs him up.

“You tell it best, babe,” says Anubis, ignoring Osiris.

“It was 1982,” she starts, looking into Anubis's eyes as he shakes his head no.

“I mean 1983.”

Another shake.

“It was sometime in the early eighties. The contras were fighting the Sandinista government in Nicaragua, and the Americans were more than willing to pay mercenaries to support the freedom-fighting contras. I first saw his tall, dark frame skulking about the local bars, clearly scouting out the merc competition. Then, that fated night on the field of battle, when he blew the head off of the nasty piece of shit who tried to get the drop on me ...” She pauses, giving Anubis a kiss.

Osiris starts to get up to leave, rolling her eyes at Ra.

“We would fight together from that moment on,” Anubis adds theatrically, swinging Isis around. “And we fight together still.” He finishes with lowering Isis into a dip, blocking Osiris's path.

“You two idiots need to get out of my way,” Osiris says with a scowl.

“Whatever you say, my queen,” jibes Anubis, slightly bowing his head and returning the scowl.

Ra brings some seriousness back to the conversation. “Well, we had our fun the other day but accomplished very little,” he says, clasping his hands in front of his chest.

Anubis straightens up and faces Ra. “We have to do the absolute unexpected to outthink this lot.”

Ra nods. “I think our best bet is to try and get hold of at least one of the two. They can't stay in the compound forever.” He taps his chin for a moment, then gestures to Isis and Anubis. “You two stay near the compound with a group of Newbies and be ready to move the minute they leave. Osiris will monitor the situation. The evolutionary timeline indicated this five-year time span; it has to be right. And these two may know the exact location from which it will flow."

CHAPTER 10

Decklan and Lauren spend the rest of the night in whispered conversations about their childhoods, including Dek's first fishing adventure with his dad—or misadventure, as it turned out, when his dog decided to bite the bait as Dek was starting his cast and got a hook stuck through his tongue; it took Dek's dad at least five long minutes of bites and curses to back the bloody hook out, after which the dog just sat there wagging his tail as the boys decided to call it a day—and Lauren's awful softball days. "I was horrible, I struck out every time I got up to hit," she tells him with a laugh. "Only to find out after I quit that I needed glasses!"

They wake early the next day expecting to feel exhausted, but having those few hours to talk intimately has them both excited about their relationship and motivates them to gain more knowledge about their situation.

"Food first, then we put a plan in play," Decklan reiterates as they head downstairs. He flips her ponytail as they walk, barely able to keep himself from touching her.

Lauren leads the way to the kitchen and runs right into the barrel chest of Brutus as she enters the doorway.

"Whoa there, little lady, you almost made me spill my smoothie," he says, his large hand covering the top of a glass of green liquid.

"Oh gosh, sorry!" stammers Lauren. She backs up a step to get a better look at the man.

Brutus is all muscle. His ebony skin contrasts beautifully with his light-blue tank top. The bandages are still on his left shoulder, but he seems to be moving fine only a day after his surgery.

"Hey guys," Cleo says, peeking around the side of Brutus. Her body was completely hidden as they entered. "Bru, this is Decklan and Lauren."

"Oh yes, nice to meet you," Brutus says with his booming voice, exchanging handshakes. "That's a cute little cabin you guys have over there in Fishing Creek Reservoir. We just missed you, apparently."

Cleo shoulders by him. "We're going to the workout room to get some rehab on his shoulder. Maybe we'll see you there later?"

Dek is wide eyed as they leave. "Wow, that's one big dude," he says. "Definitely looks like he knows his way around a workout room."

"Ah, my friends, you are up early this morning," Frenchy exclaims. He dons oven mitts and pulls a tray out of the oven. "Are you hungry? What? Of course you are hungry. Would you like some muffins?"

"Good morning, Frenchy. If you'll show me where the blender is, I think we'll make some smoothies. Brutus's looked amazing," says Lauren, peeking in the fridge for some fresh ingredients.

"I can make it for you if you like?" Frenchy asks as he retrieves the blender from the side pantry.

"That's okay," Lauren responds with a smile. "I have a special recipe that I want to try out on Dek."

Dek takes a seat at the back side of the middle island and ponders how best to accomplish what he and Lauren had agreed to earlier. After watching her for a moment, he throws caution to the wind. "Uh, Frenchy," he begins, "we were, um, thinking about doing some sightseeing and getting some lunch. Is there any place you would recommend?" Even though they have been treated more like guests than prisoners, they are well aware that they haven't really been given the okay to leave the premises.

Frenchy's expression falters slightly, then returns to its regular brightness. "Well, I'm not sure that's a great idea," he says, a touch uneasily. "With Cleo and Brutus just recently being attacked, it may not be safe."

Hoping not to raise alarm with the idea of them leaving, Lauren quickly chimes in. "Hmm, you may be right. I guess we aren't used to thinking like that. The way we've been treated here feels more like a vacation rather than protection."

Dek and Lauren exchange quiet looks as they finish their smoothies, then walk out on the veranda to get some sun. Dek leans over and gives Lauren a small kiss on the shoulder. "I know it's risky, clearly there are people in this town who are looking for us, but I think we need a minute away from here," he whispers, snuggling into her hair.

She turns to kiss him, using her hair to shield their faces. "I do too. Once we have had some time away to discuss, we may just decide this is the safest place and come back, but I think it should be our decision." She pulls back, laughing like he did something silly.

They surreptitiously peer back into the kitchen and notice that Frenchy has left the immediate vicinity. They decide to walk around the compound and get the lay of the land, paying attention to where everyone is located so they can make their escape. At around eleven o'clock they notice a group gathering.

"I think they're having a meeting. Almost all of them are now in the front dining room," Lauren whispers to Dek. "I think now is our chance."

They get up and walk casually through the garden toward the gate they had identified earlier that morning. The iron gate creaks a bit as they jump over. Quickly pulling their hoodies over their heads, they walk briskly toward the Battery about three blocks, then turn back toward the main part of town, trying to stay close to the shoreline. When they get closer to the commercial part of the downtown, they make a series of turns, finally cutting down a small, cobblestoned alley. About midway down the alley, they finally stop moving and glance around carefully, trying to determine if they were followed. Lauren gently pushes Dek back up against a wall and pretends to be making out with him.

"I didn't hear or see anyone following us," Dek whispers into Lauren's ear.

"They are way too good, and that was way too easy. I think they definitely know we've gone and are probably following us right now. The question is, are they trusting us or waiting to grab us right back up?" she whispers back.

"I'm half waiting to hear the tapping of a little cane along these cobblestones," Decklan adds with a dry laugh.

Lauren pulls back and again looks up and down the alley. "Bloody Alley," she says randomly.

Dek shoots her an odd look.

She gently takes his chin in her hand, turning his face toward a sign hanging on the stone wall behind him. "That sign says we are in Bloody Alley, the site of a historic duel."

Dek pushes off the wall to take a closer look. "It says it's still haunted. I guess we're going sightseeing after all," he jokes, finally relaxing a little. "Well, if we *do* hear a tapping cane, it might just be a ghost."

Lauren laughs and bumps his shoulder with hers. "Let's go get some lunch, and try and enjoy our time out."

He throws his arm over her shoulder and nuzzles her cheek. "The magazine in our room had an article about local historic restaurants. The Flying Tiger is just a few blocks from here. Want to try that?" he suggests.

"Sounds good."

Arm in arm, they make their way to the restaurant. As Dek opens the door, an elderly woman coming in behind them trips up the step. She gives a startled yelp as she begins to fall, but Lauren grabs her with superfast hands and stops her descent to the concrete. When the woman regains her balance and composure, she thanks Lauren profusely and apologizes for the "hullabaloo" before going to find a table.

Lauren looks at Dek wide eyed. "I can't believe I did that," she whispers, in awe of her speed.

Dek chuckles quietly as they walk to a small table near the back. Though the Tiger is pretty quiet at this time of day, just winding down from the lunch rush, they want to avoid being in the main flow of people. They pick up their menus and begin to discuss all the delicious options.

***

Osiris pulls her white SUV to a stop in front of the Flying Tiger. She cranes her neck to peer into the restaurant, trying to confirm what she thinks she just saw—the targets, alone. She grabs her phone and dials Anubis.

"You guys have got to get back here now!" she whispers aggressively. "I just ran into our Evos … alone! I'm not sure what they are thinking, but we have an opportunity here."

"What?" Anubis says incredulously. "You have got to be kidding? Shit! I'm like thirty minutes away."

Osiris curses under her breath and starts rapidly tapping her fingers on the gearshift. "Okay, are there any Newbies nearby? I think I can put them down, but I cannot get them out without help."

"I'm texting now to get someone over to you," Anubis's distant voice informs her. The call grows silent for a moment. "Done," he says. "Listen, we won't have much time before our friends arrive, if they are not there already. Start your move. I'm on my way."

Osiris gets out of the car, yanking her blond hair free from its ponytail and putting on a pair of glasses. She walks in and locates Dek and Lauren at a small table facing the street. She orders three bottled beers from the bartender, cunningly slips pills into two of them, and walks up to her marks.

"Oh my god, you absolutely saved that woman just now!" Osiris gushes at them, her deceptive emotions masked. "It is so rare to see people willingly help each other, I just had to buy you each a beer!" She puts their bottles on the table and takes a sip of her untainted beer.

"Thanks, but it was really no big deal," says Lauren, angling her beer toward Dek to cheers.

"It was! Thank you for being decent humans," Osiris says with a big, friendly smile. "Y'all have a good day now." She goes back to the front of the restaurant and shoots off a text—*You guys have about fifteen minutes to get here*—then sits back in her chair, waiting and watching the door.

"That was so nice," Lauren says, sliding her hand over to Dek's.

After the waitress stops by to take their order, they finish their beers and chat freely as they wait for lunch to be served.

"I'm not sure what they're all so worried about," Lauren says, lounging back in her chair. "I have a hard time believing that whatever we do or wherever we go, we're in imminent danger. You?"

Dek chokes back a laugh and holds a hand over his mouth to avoid spitting out his beer. He wonders if Lauren is feeling a bit tipsy or if this is simply her personality when she's completely relaxed—a state he hasn't experienced much of yet due to their chaotic circumstances.

"I don't think the Children have given our genius brains enough credit," Lauren adds with a mischievous smile. She taps her forehead. "I worked my tail off in school to get my thinker in this fabulous, tip-top shape. I bet you did too!"

"Your 'thinker'?" Decklan chuckles. "Well, I certainly worked hard, but I'm not sure my gray matter is as topflight as yours!"

She flicks his hand. "You flatter me."

Decklan, glancing out a side window, feels an odd pang in his gut. "So I don't know if people are actively looking for us," he says warily, "but I actually feel kind of nervous at the thought. Crazy things do keep happening to us ...."

Lauren nods, then waves her hand around the restaurant. "To all these people, though, we're just a normal, young couple out on a lunch date."

"Normal?" Dek repeats with a laugh. "Just think, if we have the potential to live for two hundred years, we are just getting started. How's that for bonkers?"

"It's like, well, we've been given another lifetime ... it's a lot to get your arms around."

Two men in their thirties enter the restaurant and grab seats at the bar.

A minute later, Lauren sits up straighter.

Dek whispers, "Uh, do you hear that?"

"Yeah," Lauren replies, hearing the buzzing around them. Her adrenaline spikes. "We need to get out of here."

"Fuckin' intuition," Dek swears under his breath. He looks for another way out of the restaurant as Lauren throws some cash down on the table, and they both stand to leave.

Lauren sways and has to put her hands on the back of the chair to steady herself. "Oh shit!" she says, her voice sounding like an echo in her ears. "Dek, I think I've been drugged ...."

Dek steadies himself by holding the wall. "Dammit ... me too," he says weakly.

Osiris and the men at the bar start to walk over. Dek tries to lunge at them but feebly falls to his knees.

Lauren pushes back from the table, away from the approaching group. "Stay away from me!" she shakily yells. "Help! Someone help!"

An older man sitting alone at a nearby booth stands up, prompting one of the two men to say, "Look, man, stay out of this. We're cops. We have this under control ...."

The man starts to return to his seat, then bursts forward like lightning. He kicks the first man so hard in the face that he nearly takes his head off. The second man is quick to react. Pushing Osiris out of the way, he tackles the man from the booth and sends them both crashing over a table.

Time is up, Osiris thinks. *I can't take both Evos ... the man is heavier but closer to me.* She jumps into action, grabbing Dek in a fireman's carry and hurrying for the door. Beeping her SUV doors open, she throws Dek across the back seats and climbs over him to the driver's side. She starts the ignition and looks over to see the man from the booth slamming a Newbie into the wall and starting for the door. Osiris screeches out into traffic, passing Anubis and

Isis coming to her aid. She starts to smile at the idea of them kicking that guy's ass, when another car slams into hers, almost causing her to lose the wheel. She quickly glances over at the other driver, then hard cuts the wheel and sends the other car into a group of parked cars on the side of the road.

"I guess she didn't need our help," Anubis says to Isis, proudly watching Osiris speed past in the opposite direction. The words are barely out of his mouth when he hears the collision behind them. Looking back, he sees Osiris's truck slam against another car. He turns front and sees multiple vehicles pulling up outside the Tiger. "Get us the hell outta here."

The man from the booth reenters the Tiger and scoops Lauren up in his arms. He glances over at the two unconscious men as he walks out the door. Two cars pull up. Thi Thi jumps out of an SUV driven by Alexander and helps the man ease Lauren into the back seat.

"Let's go before the cops get here," the man says as he hops in beside Lauren, rubbing his face and slowly looking more like Philippe. "Osiris got Decklan," he says heavily. "Luckily, she only had a couple of Newbie stooges with her, or they might have gotten them both."

"We never should have allowed them to go out on their own," Alexander says ruefully. "Clearly, Ra is willing to risk a lot to get ahold of them."

Philippe frowns. "I was on them *all day*," he says, bitterly emphasizing the last two words. "I don't understand how Osiris found them, or for that matter, even how she knew they left the compound."

Thi Thi looks back at him from the passenger seat. "I can hear her heart beating, but what'd they do to her?"

"I think they gave her a strong tranq," Philippe says. He feels her pulse. "Steady .... She may be out for a few hours, but I think she'll be fine."

"And what of her boyfriend?" Thi Thi prompts gently.

"Ra wouldn't want to kill him before getting a chance to extract some information first," Alexander quietly chimes in. "After that, if Dek doesn't want to join Ra's cause, he could be used as a blood bag for the creation of Newbies. Dek still has a high viral load in his blood, and Ra always needs soldiers."

They fall silent.

Alexander's knuckles whiten as his grip tightens on the wheel. "We'll get him back before that, though," he grits out.

CHAPTER 11

Lauren groggily cracks open her eyes, then quickly closes them as the bright fluorescent lights sting. "Ugh," she groans, reaching up and rubbing her sore eyes. "What happened?"

"Well, you decided to go sightseeing, despite our recommendation that you remain here," a man responds wryly. "And you were almost kidnapped as a result." He is sitting next to her bed, but the bright lights behind him shadow his face. "It's good to see that you're coming around. The Evos use tranquilizers that are formulated to put down even the evolved for a good amount of time."

Lauren continues to lie back, hands over her eyes, trying to process the words that he's saying. Then the memories come seeping in, and she springs up onto her elbow. "Dek?" she yells. She immediately grabs her head in agony. "Shit!"

"Take it easy," the man says, placing a gentle hand on her shoulder. "The effects will take some time to wear off."

"I've been with Dek for almost every minute since we evolved. There is a certain sound that his cells make, kind of a calming hum …. He isn't here, is he?" A tear drips down her cheek.

The man slowly shakes his head. "He was taken by the woman who spiked your drinks," he tells her. "Osiris. She's one of Ra's top people."

"We have to get him back." Lauren looks up, and her vision of the man sitting next to her bed finally clears. She is surprised to see that it's Philippe, someone who has barely had any contact with her since their first day.

"We will get him back," he replies, his tone brooking no argument. "Maria is already using various cameras around the city to track Osiris. Carson rammed her car trying to stop her getaway, and that damage is easy to identify as we look for the vehicle."

"I want to help." Lauren starts to get up, only to feel dizzy and fall back onto the pillow. Another tear rolls down her cheek.

"We got this," Philippe assures her. "Rest now, until you feel better. It will take a couple of days for us to find him and put together a plan, but if you really want to be part of the recovery team, I'll help you train once you've regained your strength."

She leans back up on her elbow, steadier this time. "I should be good to go after a shower and some food," she says with a determined look.

"I'll meet you in the gym in two hours, if you're up to it," he says, walking toward the door.

"Hey," she calls out, sitting up on the side of the bed. "It was you, the man in the Tiger, who fought off the other guys?"

He glances back at her and nods. "I was on you both from the time you jumped over the fence," he admits. His eyes drop to the ground and he shakes his head regretfully. "I just couldn't react fast enough to save you both."

"Thank you, for saving me," she says, looking up at him.

"I promise I'll do better next time," he says, gently closing the door.

***

The shower works miracles. Lauren takes her time, allowing the hot water to ease her achy muscles. Putting on her tank top and yoga pants, she feels the spring in her step returning and heads up to the veranda to get a quick hit of sunlight. Frenchy and Urvinder are out there enjoying some tea and catching the last rays of the afternoon as she walks out.

"Ah! My friend, you are feeling better?" Frenchy asks, raising his arms in welcome.

"Much better, thank you," Lauren says, walking over to the railing and raising her face to the sky. "The sun feels great. I'm glad I wasn't too late to catch it."

"You must be famished," says Frenchy, quickly getting to his feet. "I have just the thing. Give me about fifteen minutes; I promise I will not disappoint." He hurries toward the door.

"Come," Urvinder beckons. "Keep me company for the last few minutes of daylight."

Lauren makes her way over and sits across from the older woman. Urvinder keeps her gaze trained on Lauren the whole time, continuing to assess her.

"You're not going to freeze me again, are you?" Lauren jokes uneasily.

Urvinder ignores the dig. "You were lucky. Your youth helped you to metabolize the tranquilizer faster," she tells Lauren coolly. "But you lost your friend?"

Strain creeps across Lauren's face. "Yes, the uh, the Evos took him." She pauses for a beat. "This is all so confusing," she hastily adds, with a brisk shake of her head. "What could they want from us? We barely know what's happening to us, let alone anything of value."

Urvinder watches her intently. "They think you know the location of where your virus came from. They are looking to cause the ninth evolution," she says calmly, holding her steaming cup near her mouth before taking another sip.

Lauren turns to her with an astonished look on her face. "Huh? The ninth evolution? And why does where the virus came from have anything to do with it?" Knees bouncing, Lauren blows out a deep breath. "I was the one working on the experiment .... Dek doesn't know what the samples were or where they were from. He won't be able to answer their questions."

Urvinder sets her cup down on the saucer. "Sounds like they got the wrong one," she says with a glimmer of a smile.

"Alexander never mentioned the ninth evolution."

"It's not his favorite subject," Urvinder says without elaborating.

Annoyance flashes across Lauren's face. "Would *you* care to share something about it then?" she asks.

Urvinder continues to gaze serenely at Lauren. "I think I like you," she says. "You seem like a strong, astute woman."

The corner of Lauren's mouth twitches up. *High praise coming from someone who has lived for almost two hundred years,* she thinks.

Leaning forward, Urvinder folds her hands on the table. "There is a theory, Ra's theory, that there are many evolutionary jumps—times where the planet evolves faster than natural selection would allow. Ra believes that the evolutions happen, are happening, at decreasing intervals. According to his timeline, we are nearing the time for the ninth evolution."

Lauren's forehead wrinkles as she processes the information. "What is the basis of his theory? Where does his timeline even begin? Because based on current evolutionary theory—"

Urvinder pats her hand and smoothly interjects. "Ra has been researching the timeline for many years and believes that the first evolutionary jump was millions of years ago. According to his research, the times between evolutionary jumps are getting smaller each jump, by a factor of pi."

"The number pi, as in 3.14, et cetera?"

Urvinder nods. "Not all of the jumps are equally significant," she continues. "Some are just small changes to brain size or ability to learn, but Ra thinks it is time for the ninth, and he is ready to help make it happen." She sits back to gauge Lauren's reaction.

"Help make it happen?" Lauren asks, her scientific mind firing on all cylinders. "Did *someone* help make the other eight evolutions happen?" She shakes her head, growing as animated as she is intrigued. "I can't believe people would have been able to do anything like that thousands of years ago."

Urvinder smiles patiently. "Ra believes the evolutionary virus is released differently each jump. This time, man has the ability to actually cause the release. In the past, the virus may have been unleashed due to a meteor strike or a shift in tectonic plates."

"But wait … if the virus has the potential to kill half of the people in the world," Lauren says, her voice rising, "how could he just decide himself that it's time to release it?"

"It is a very complex moral issue," Urvinder agrees solemnly. "Ra has his own reasons and justifications, even besides that of his timeline, telling him that now is the time."

Lauren leaps up and begins pacing. "What if his theory is wrong?" she asks, biting her thumbnail. "What if each time an evolutionary jump occurred, it was just due to chance, and this doesn't need to happen yet?"

"His insistence that he is correct is what drove him away from us, taking a small group of like-minded people with him," Urvinder replies calmly.

Lauren looks over at the doorway. Amid the wafts of onions and seasonings coming from deep inside the house, she senses Frenchy coming their way.

Urvinder smiles. "You are starting to adjust to your other heightened senses now, aren't you? Hearing the noises from inside, feeling the vibrations of Frenchy's footsteps on the floor. Soon it will be second nature, not something that you are surprised by."

Frenchy pops out of the doorway a few moments later. "Food is up," he says, placing an aromatic steak sandwich in front of Lauren.

"That looks divine," Urvinder says, standing and collecting her belongings. "Eat while it's hot, and we'll continue our chat another time."

"Thank you, Urvinder. You've been very helpful." Lauren turns her attention to the sandwich, her mouth full-on watering. "This looks and smells amazing, Frenchy. Thank you. I will apologize ahead for absolutely tearing into it."

He smiles. "I hope that dear Urvinder was not upsetting you too much?" he asks, watching her devour the meal.

She pauses a moment between chews. "I'm no more upset than I already was, just worried that Ra is gonna hurt Dek."

"I've known Ra since the 1950s .... He is headstrong and passionate, but he is not evil. Whereas Alexander's interests lie more on the currently evolved, Ra has always been focused on those who will be evolved. I wouldn't put it past him to sacrifice the few for the many, but if Dek can serve a purpose toward his ultimate goal, he should be safe."

She shrugs helplessly. "If his ultimate goal is the ninth evolution, I don't know if Dek has the knowledge to be of help."

CHAPTER 12

Isis gently pats Dek on the cheek. "Wakey wakey, love."

Decklan slowly raises a hand to his forehead, his eyes still shut. "Oh my god, Lauren. I feel like I've been run over by a truck," he moans. Groggy from the sedative, he rubs his eyes and glances at the chair across from the bed. He does a double take as Isis's dark curly hair and mahogany skin come into focus. "Shit …."

"How's your head feeling?" Isis asks with a sadistic smile. "Osiris's drugs kick like a mule."

"Is Lauren here? Is she okay—?"

"She is fine and will remain that way as long as you cooperate," Isis lies, quickly calming her emotional response to conceal the deception.

"Don't harm her. I'll give you whatever you want, or what I can, I guess." After a short pause, he adds, "What *do* you want?"

A man enters the room and sits next to the woman. "I see our guest has awoken."

Dek pegs him to be about five eleven, in good physical shape, with the posture of an army officer. His graying hair is cut military short and his piercing blue eyes seem to spark in anticipation.

"My name is Victor Roska, but most of my people refer to me as Ra. This beautiful woman next to me is Isis."

Dek sits back in the bed. "I've heard of you .... You were involved in the gunfight in the Market, I believe, looking for us?"

"Well, yes, I was not personally there, but my dear Isis played a role," Ra says jovially, encouraged by Dek's willingness to talk.

Isis leans forward, placing her elbows on her knees. "How's my big friend Brutus doin'? A few inches higher and I wouldn't have to ask," she says and gives Dek a wide-eyed smile.

Dek looks at her with disdain.

"All that hoopla, but it seems we were able to arrange a meeting after all," Ra says with a satisfied sigh.

"Well, I'll take Alexander's form of kidnapping any day over whatever it was that you placed in my drink," Dek says, pressing his palms into his eyes. "So what is it exactly that you want with us?"

"Did Alexander not tell you about me and my wants?" Ra asks peevishly. Not waiting for an answer, he states matter-of-factly, "I want the ninth evolution."

Dek stares blankly at him. He raises his hands and shrugs. "Nope, not a clue."

Ra, clearly exasperated, glances over at Isis in disbelief. He internally listens to Dek's vital signs and knows that Dek is telling the truth.

"Is it the evolution that happened to us?" Dek asks, taking a wild guess.

"Yes," Ra says. "According to the pi timeline, the ninth evolution's full release date is upon us." He picks imaginary lint off his pants before looking back at Decklan. "Sometime in the next few months, the virus will be discharged ... and the chosen ones will be saved."

Dek inhales sharply and takes a moment to gather his thoughts. With painstaking slowness, as if speaking to a child, he says, "From the small sample size of studies that we did ... we ascertained that over half the population would be killed .... You can't possibly want that?"

"Why, yes," Ra responds bluntly. "This is how the world will replenish itself." He stands and walks around the room, punctuating his next points by ticking them off on his fingers. "One, a reduced population and the cellular enhancements of the ninth evolution will make a world free of hunger and rich in natural resources. Two, our increased intelligence levels will allow communications and understanding on a level the world has never seen."

"If this is the ninth evolution, by your count, then I think the world may have seen this before. Maybe when the eighth evolution occurred," Dek quips back in response.

"Each evolution is different. Giving the world only what it needs to get to the next one," Ra explains. "Some of the evolutions were small, having minimal overall gain but no less necessary to the big picture."

"And what is the big picture?" Dek asks.

"Why, the final and most advanced form that our bodies can take," Ra says fervently.

Ra's undisguised zeal reminds Dek a bit of Alexander. *But their intentions could not be more different*, he thinks as he slowly gets to his full height and takes some tentative steps around the room. "So what happens then? We just continue on our merry ways, living our best lives, not thinking of the billions who died getting us here?" Dek asks, not even trying to hide how sickened he is by Ra's disregard for human life.

"If the evolutions do not complete the full cycle of the species development, then all life on this planet is worthless anyway," Ra claims.

"No world and no person is worthless," Dek spits back.

"A world laid to waste and a completely dead population, which could occur before the ninth is released, is just a worthless hunk of rock floating in the cosmos," Isis pipes in.

"What are you talking about?" replies Dek, his voice straining with frustration.

Ra shoves off the wall and puts his hand on Dek's shoulder to keep him still. "Did Alexander ever bother telling you why I am no longer a member of his little group?"

Silence.

"He probably made me out to be a bloodthirsty villain, didn't he?" Again he pauses and reads Dek's silence as a response. "That's the familiarity you gain from knowing someone for over a hundred years," he says dryly. "Well, I'll tell you that we encountered the virus together at a small village in Africa and eventually found others like us. We studied the virus, its effects, and we searched for the source, mainly with the intent of containing it for the exact fear you are expressing, the death of millions of innocent people, which of course today would be billions—"

"And now you are trying to bring on Armageddon?" Dek interjects, shoving Ra's hand from his shoulder.

Ignoring the outburst, Ra continues. "Shortly after the end of the Second World War, where once again man had done the unthinkable and let greed, hate, and jealousy cause the deaths of millions, Darley and I were working on an evolutionary timeline, trying to find a pattern to the evolutionary jumps. So often in this world there are patterns entrenched in all things. Searching old documents and troves of fossilized archaeologic records, we discovered that in generalized terms there was a pattern to the leaps. The pattern was a countdown of sorts where the time lapse between the leaps was decreasing by a multiple of pi."

Dek puts his hand up. "Wait. You're saying that the jumps are happening more frequently over time?"

"Yes, a countdown," Isis says excitedly. "And to our best calculation the next jump, after the ninth, would be happening in about thirty or forty years. The fact that pi never ends and time is a relative concept made it hard to pinpoint exactly, but that time window is now."

Dek sits down heavily on the bed. Looking for an angle for his argument, he asks, "So if it's going to happen anyway, why are you working to hurry it along?"

Ra nods in understanding. "Well, we initially had planned on just sitting back and waiting for it to happen," he explains. "In the 1960s a new problem came to light. After the Cuban Missile Crisis I realized that we may not make it to the next jump. The technological advancements of humans have given them the ability to wipe out all life on the planet. The next evolutionary jump would allow for advanced thinking and understanding and a surplus of food and resources. The next jump could prevent the wars of the past from reoccurring if we could just make it."

Dek's eyes narrow as he begins to understand Ra's thought process. "You want to cause the next evolutionary jump to prevent World War III?"

"Not just World War III," he says, angling himself next to Dek on the bed. "I believe that the timing of these jumps is set to mimic the development of the species. The jumps don't just occur because the pi timeline is up. They are designed to happen when the planet needs them to happen for its overall survival. The easiest one to see is the one that took out the dinosaurs and set the stage for the coming of man. If the dinosaurs had not been wiped out, this planet would not have been suitable for early man to survive. Subsequent jumps have all been leading up to what we are as a species today."

"So you have your timeline telling you when these jumps are about to occur, but you believe that this timeline is also based on knowledge of how our species will develop, use resources, and become a danger to ourselves?" asks Dek. "That's a bit of a stretch, don't you think? How could that be possible?"

Ra sighs and rubs the back of his neck. "I have some theories, but I will know more after the jump." He stands and walks to the door. "I do know that it's not as simple as that. We are also polluting the environment and creating increasingly virulent diseases and viruses. If the jump doesn't happen soon, we could have irreparable damage to the ecosystem or a worldwide pandemic that could also wipe us out. When you think about how many people will not survive the next evolution, you need to take into account how many others will survive cancers or other medical conditions that would have killed them if they hadn't evolved ...."

Isis stands up and walks toward Ra. "At the end of the day," she says, "the threat of total annihilation is around every corner.

The evolution is really the only thing that will save this planet and this species."

Ra nods in agreement. "The virus has already begun to leak out in small doses. Will we wait until maybe it's too late, or do we cause this to happen and save as many people as we can?" He looks at Dek intently, like a lawyer trying to judge if the jury has accepted his closing arguments as fact.

"I can see your point," Dek says slowly. "And I understand how you could come to this conclusion, but you are making these decisions for people who don't have these theories or any of this knowledge. They will be giving up their loved ones or maybe their own lives. It may be the right way to go, I don't really know. I have to think hard about some ideas that I was quite sure about. In the end, though, doesn't everyone deserve the same chance to put their two cents in the mix and find a solution for everyone?"

"Bah!" scoffs Ra, waving his hand. "We have been given this gift early to lead the rest of the sheep, whether it is to become our equals or if it is to the slaughterhouse." He turns at a tap on the door.

Anubis comes in with a tray of food. He walks over to the left side of Dek's bed and lifts a tray stand up and across Dek's lap. He takes Dek's left hand and, quick as a viper, slaps a handcuff around Dek's wrist and the bar attached to the bed. "Enjoy your food, mate." He flashes Dek a grin and walks back into the hallway, Ra behind him, and Isis closing the door behind them.

"Wait!" Dek yells, straining his arm against the cuff. "You can't just keep me here like this!"

"The cuffs and the whole bed system are reinforced to keep even evolved people tied up," Isis says over her shoulder. "Just relax, pretty boy. We'll come back and see you soon."

CHAPTER 13

Wham! The glass to the workout room shakes and quivers as Lauren's spin throws Philippe into the padded wall of the training area. Hopping back and forth on the balls of her feet, fists up in a defensive posture, Lauren smiles down on his crumpled form. "Is that what you were talking about? Hip throw?" she says, giving him a little sass.

"Uh, yeah, I think that was definitely a form of it," he replies, groaning and getting to his feet. As soon as he sees her relax her stance, he launches himself at her like a lion on its prey. Grabbing her left wrist and spinning under her arm from behind, he puts her in a choke hold before grabbing hold of her other wrist. "Now that would be how you quickly recover advantage from said hip throw," he taunts, before releasing her.

"Wow, that was so fast," she says, pausing to get a drink of water.

"You should be able to be even faster than me, once you have fully learned how to maximize your evolved body," he replies, toweling off his face. "Speed and flexibility will be the best fit for your body type. You can't overwhelm opponents with strength and brute force like Carson or Brutus. Your body will do what you need it to do naturally, but you must concentrate and train your response. More than ever, the mind-and-body connection is true once you have evolved. Your mind, calling on your body, takes an attack move down to the smallest nuances: the fast twitch of your muscle fibers, hardening of the bones for a strike, enhanced nerve conduction speeding up all your movements—all of these evolved bodily functions can be brought into play."

"That was a pretty slick move. I felt like I barely had a target to focus on, let alone strike," she begrudgingly admits.

"I call that one the serpent's coil," he says with a laugh. "It is a combination of explosive speed and body flexibility. Relaxing certain tendons, I can almost coil around you like a striking snake evading your defense. You thought I would come at you more directly rather than attack you from behind. It is one of my favorite moves. It also works well for impressing a woman at a club. One minute you are approaching her seductively, the next you are whispering in her ear."

"For an old guy, I'll bet you do just fine trying to pick up women in the club," Lauren says with a wink.

"Old guy?" he says, taken aback. "I'm only fifty-eight, just a baby in this crew."

Lauren sets down her water and resumes her fighting stance.

"I think we have had enough fight training for now," says Philippe, holding up his hands. "Now we stretch and meditate, allowing our mind and flushed muscles to come together." They walk over to a softer padded area with large windows looking out into the lush green garden.

"Let your mind guide your cells to healing the taxed muscle fibers," he says, motioning for Lauren to sit on the mat. "Stretch out your right leg and feel your muscles relax into the stretch." He applies slight pressure to her back, deepening the stretch. After about ten seconds, he tells her to switch to the other leg, again applying pressure to her back to deepen the stretch. "That's it," he whispers, his head nearing her ear.

"Yes, please take a seat over there, Romeo," she says, straightening her back and stretching her neck.

Philippe, aghast, sits down next to her. "Are you insinuating that I am hitting on you?"

"I am," she says, looking at him with eyebrows raised.

A wry smile creeps across his face. "Maybe a little," he says, shrugging his shoulders.

"A little? Touching my back, whispering in my ear, and you kicked up the pheromones quite a bit as well," she says, pointing to her nose. "I'm flattered, but not interested. Our focus needs to be on Dek."

"You are still thinking like the unevolved," Philippe says with a long, prevailed-upon sigh. "Your life is just beginning. You are in your twenties with a life expectancy in the two hundreds. The term 'get out and live a little' takes on a whole new meaning. You will have many lovers over this time. The need to tie yourself to one will become an antiquated idea. Life is about experiencing, sensing, and feeling; it would be a shame to limit that, don't you think?"

"Sorry, not going to work, but nice try," she says with a grin. She shifts over on the mats to face him. "So what's your story anyway? How did you, uh, change?"

Philippe smiles. He does enjoy talking about his life. He leans over his extended leg in a stretch. "I was born in a small town just outside of Paris in 1965, but when I was in high school, I was offered a work-study opportunity in a Canadian children's camp. We would go to a nearby stream and collect rock samples. We'd bring them back and clean them so the kids had 'treasure' to take home. One of the samples had a piece of radioactive metal stuck on it and after we cleaned up the sample, a small amount of virus was released. It killed the child I was working with and changed me. The horrible death of the child forced the camp to close, but I later found out the owners imported discarded materials from South American mines to ensure the riverbed had plenty of samples for the kids. This seemed to be the source of our viral interaction. Later, I went to some South American cities trying to track down the source and get some answers about what happened to me. That was when Alexander found me, buzzing away at a bus stop near Mexico City, as he likes to say it."

"Interesting," Lauren says. "Is it not at all possible the virus came from a Canadian stream?"

Philippe shakes his head. "After learning so much in the past thirty to forty years, I think we all believe that the virus is contained in the Earth's crust somewhere close to the equator. That way it has the maximum exposure to sunlight the minute it comes out. The sunlight causes the virus to become airborne and highly infective. If our theories about viral evolution are correct, the equator would be the location affording the most sunlight at the time of a large-scale release."

She puts her hand on his shoulder. "Wait. What do you mean 'large-scale release'?"

"We believe that if Ra were going to cause the next evolution, he would most likely try and set off an explosion inside the Earth's crust," Philippe explains as he turns, grabs her hands, and hauls them both upright. "This would blast a large amount of viral matter into the atmosphere and separate the virus from the radioactive metal that's keeping it dormant. Add in the copious amounts of sunlight and prevailing winds, and you have global evolution."

"This is such an insane story," Lauren says, bending to pick up her water bottle and hoodie. "Like, surreal … stranger than fiction … Do you have any idea why Ra went down the, uh, dark path, for lack of a better term?"

Philippe throws his towel into his bag, hoists it to his shoulder, then nudges Lauren out the door. "Ra was still a big part of the Children of the Sun when Alexander found me," he tells her as they walk. "I was there for the whole breakup and the rift that formed between them …. Suffice it to say, Alexander always seemed more interested in finding and studying evolved people than the idea of releasing the virus on the world, or using our evolved blood to evolve others, like Ra." He pauses and takes a deep breath. "I'll admit, Ra has a strong argument, but mass murder on the scale that he's talking about … we can't be a part of that."

"Urvinder thinks Ra is after Dek and me to find out the source of our infection." Lauren peers at him. "Is that what you still do for Alexander—try to find the source of the virus?"

He shakes his head. "Actually, I am one of the lead scouts on his discovery team. When Maria or one of the other computer nerds sees something in the papers that could be a sign of a newly evolved human, I am usually sent in with a partner—in your case that was Carson—and we watch to determine if in fact it is the case or just something else."

"Huh. So when did you know we had changed?" she asks.

"When I asked you for money, disguised as a homeless man in Madison, I learned two things. One, that you both had recently evolved—I could hear your cells buzzing before I got to the car. Two, that you were beautiful and had a kind heart." He winks at her.

Lauren smiles and then wrinkles her nose. "One downside to the evolution is I can really tell when I need a shower," she says wryly.

She hears Philippe's laughter down the hall as she walks in the opposite direction to her room.

"Don't forget to meet Cleo and Brutus in the armory at two," he shouts after her.

CHAPTER 14

Especially irritated after a malfunction of his plane's landing lights caused a diversion and four-hour layover in Dallas, Mr. Helms is finally exiting plane onto the tarmac in Quito, Ecuador. The midday rains are showering down as Feldman rushes over from the car with an umbrella. He points Helms toward the car, holding the umbrella high near the top rather than at the handle.

"I hope that the flight was not too bad, sir?" he asks, opening the door with his opposite hand, causing Helms to step out of the way. Receiving no response, Feldman gently shuts the door and walks around, getting in the passenger side. "Take us to the hotel," he instructs the driver.

"No," grunts Helms sternly, glancing at the driver's eyes in the mirror. "I want to go to the camp right away. I want you to set me up in the command center with a room and office. I'll be staying there until we are fully underway. These constant trips back and forth from the States are starting to wear on my nerves. I'm ready to see this thing through."

"Yes, sir," Feldman corrects himself. "We need to be taken to the hotel parking lot where we will get a transport to take us to the dig-site camp."

They make the ten-minute drive in relative silence, with just the sounds of the raindrops and the swish of the car's wipers. Feldman quietly texts ahead to set up the transport. Getting the vibe from Helms that their conversations will need to be private, Feldman requests a vehicle with a separate compartment from the driver.

They arrive at the hotel just as their vehicle pulls into the parking lot. Helms remains in the car until everything has been moved over to the camp transport.

"Everything is ready, sir," says Feldman, poking his head in the passenger door. "I have radioed ahead to the camp to set up the command center and living quarters. It will take us a few hours to get there, and they should have most of it done when we arrive."

Helms nods and gestures for Feldman to join him in the rear compartment. As the large transport vehicle lurches to a start, Helms takes a satellite Wi-Fi hookup and his laptop out.

"Okay, Feldman, how is it really going?" Helms asks, not looking up as his computer connection links. "We now have a more secure place to talk, out of earshot of the driver, so I'd appreciate your candor."

"We are still having some troubles at the site," Feldman admits. "Little thefts and some damage to our drilling equipment. I am sure it is the local help that we have been using to speed up the process and am confident we will weed out the problem children this week. I also have finally gotten governmental clearance for the use of larger explosives. They have been ordered and should be here in a couple of weeks."

"That actually sounds better than I was expecting," Helms says. "If they keep messing with our digging equipment, then we will blow a big hole in their jungle and they will have no choice but to let us clean it up."

"With the current depth that we are digging at, the explosives should blast us almost all the way down to metal depth," Feldman confirms.

"I also wanted to check with you on our situation in North Carolina. In your last report, Summers and Thomas had vanished from the lake house. Have they been found?"

"No, sir, it seems we were too slow in sending the team in," Feldman says. He stares intently out the window but can feel Helms's heated gaze on him. "The Heretic Group has not had any success in locating them, but their car was found in a parking garage in Charlotte. They may have been seeking a lawyer's help, but that is speculation."

Helms cuts to the chase. "So, bottom line, they are gone and we have no idea where they are?"

Feldman purses his lips and nods.

Helms sighs. "Okay, have the Heretics send a couple of guys down here. We may have need of their expertise if we can't get the locals to settle down. That will be a better use of their time."

"Yes, sir, I will send them a communiqué when we arrive at camp."

Tapping rapidly on his keyboard, Helms says, "I am pulling up my notes on Vincent's reports now ...." He quickly scans the monitor. "Right, so Vincent initially reported that Thomas had almost half of his hand cut off in the lab accident. Around a week later, he then reported that Thomas was performing some kind of high-intensity workouts, with no mention of hand injury. What do you make of that?"

Feldman shrugs. "I don't know, sir, maybe 'half his hand' was exaggerated. Although, Mr. Vincent was never one to embellish much."

"I actually looked over some of the medical records that Vincent took from the hospital while covering up the mess," Helms says, turning his computer screen and showing a hand X-ray missing the ring and pinkie fingers. "And the doctor indicated the loss of two fingers on the left hand in his notes."

"That is baffling," Feldman says carefully. "Sounds like someone had to be exaggerating somewhere."

"The report also said they both passed out when the lab accident occurred, but it didn't give a solid reason why," Helms adds.

"I did hear that," Feldman says, nodding his head.

"These two scientists somehow managed to escape and elude one of my best people, time and time again. This literally makes no sense to me," Helms says, still reading the report on his computer.

"If what's in the report is true, then Thomas would have had to do all that with one hand," adds Feldman.

"Richard did say in one of his reports that they were trying to figure out something that had happened to them. Of course that idiot just blew it off as if it were of no consequence," Helms says quietly. He shoots Feldman a scornful look, then slowly turns to peer out the window, rubbing his thumb over his bottom lip as if something just occurred to him.

CHAPTER 15

Lauren finishes up her shower and ducks outside her room, planning to run down to the kitchen to ask Frenchy how to get to the armory. Apparently, Philippe was a step ahead of her, leaving a small hand-drawn map on a note tacked to her door.

The map is easy to follow, leading her down a wide concrete stairwell into the basement. She can hear the sound of muffled gunfire as she walks down the dimly lit hallway. She comes to the door and reads the sign on it: PLEASE TURN ON LIGHT SWITCH AND WAIT FOR TWO MINUTES BEFORE ENTERING. Lauren flicks the light switch and steps back. The gunfire stops and the door opens from the inside. The large frame of Brutus moves aside, welcoming Lauren in. "We were just getting in some warm-up shots," he tells her. His deep, comforting voice and Australian accent put her a little more at ease in this unfamiliar situation.

The armory is a narrow room, about ten by twenty. On the wall immediately across from the door and wrapping around the rear are backlit glass cabinets filled with a large variety of firearms hanging on hooks. The lower part of the display is lined with drawers, looking like a fancy curio furniture piece. There is a metal table with a padded top to one side of the door and the other side has a half wall topped with a plexiglass barrier and an access door. Through the plexiglass, Lauren can see Cleo, wearing shooting glasses and a pair of earmuffs, adjusting the scope on a compact automatic rifle. She is standing at a small table with a long concrete tunnel in front of her, culminating in two targets on separate conveyors. Cleo looks up and waves to Lauren as she approaches the glass.

"Well, it didn't take you guys long to make quick work of those targets," Lauren says as the targets roll forward, both with the faces shot completely out of them.

"Have you ever done this before?" asks Brutus, taking a smaller-sized pistol out of a drawer, along with a box of ammunition.

"Can't say that I've had the want or need to up to this point," Lauren replies.

Cleo walks in from the shooting tunnel. "Girl, you don't know what you've been missing. I would have never thought it growing up in a gunless household, but I love the feel of cold hard steel in my hand and of lighting up that target. What did you pick out for her, Bru?"

"I reckon we'll start with something small and work our way up," he says to Cleo. Turning to Lauren, he adds, "You're a smart girl. Let me run through some quick safety training and you can get rolling in the tunnel."

For the next half hour, Cleo coaches Lauren on shooting technique. Lauren trains on and fires six different types of firearms, starting with the smaller pistol and finishing with the automatic compact rifle that Cleo was using when she first came into the room.

"I don't know if I'm going to be spending all my free time down here turning these targets into confetti, but it actually was kind of fun," says Lauren as she sets down the rifle and starts the conveyor rolling her target back to her. She takes off the earmuffs and holds up the target for inspection.

"You're a natural," yells Brutus through the glass, giving her a thumbs-up.

Cleo takes off her ear protection and peers back at Lauren through the large hole shot out of the target. "Good job! I think you will be able to hold your own in a firefight now."

They clean up the practice range and walk over to Brutus, who is cleaning firearms.

"Thank you so much for taking the time to instruct me. I really appreciate it," says Lauren.

"I think Cleo just wanted an excuse to hit the range," jokes Brutus.

"I keep picturing that crazy bitch Isis every time I shoot. I'm going to get her back for hurting you," Cleo says, touching Brutus's still-bandaged shoulder.

"I'll be all right, love," he responds. "If she was a better shot, we may not be able to say that."

"What exactly happened the other day?" asks Lauren. "I know you got shot, but was it all just for Ra to get hold of Dek and me?"

"Yup, as far as we know," Cleo says. "Bru and I were heading to pick you guys up at the lake house, but Urvinder nabbed you first."

"Our guess is that my old pal Anubis and Isis were supposed to intercept us and then take you two back to Ra," Brutus adds.

"Wait, were you really friends with Anubis?" Lauren asks incredulously. "Like, another Ra–Alexander situation?"

"Anubis and I go way back. We actually met Ra and Alexander together," says Brutus, carefully placing another pistol back in its case. "He was just plain old Cal Richards back then." He stops and looks at Lauren. "You really want to hear this?"

"Yup," she says, loudly popping the *p*. "I want to hear everything!" She leans her back against the wall and gestures for him to continue.

He chuckles. "Okay ... well, we grew up in the same neighborhood and constantly tried to find a hustle to make us a little coin. Sometime after World War II, we encountered the virus. We ran across a group of smugglers who were moving some semiprecious stones and metals. They needed a bit of muscle, and we needed a bit of money. Both Cal and I were evolved by our exposure to the virus, but those other blokes didn't fare so well with it. We took what we could of the jewels and left them to be found by the cops. We used the money that we got from selling some of the jewels to get out of Australia. The police couldn't get us for murder 'cause those blokes had died of cancer, but we had some of the jewels still and weren't about to stay around to find out if they'd be after us for theft. Most of the jewels had come from Africa, so we decided to go there to unload the rest. It was actually Cal who first met Victor, trying to move some jewels in the marketplace in Cairo. Cal had a crazy idea to steal some art pieces from Victor and Alexander's warehouse, which went terribly bad, but eventually got us added to the group."

"Victor?" asks Lauren.

"Victor Roska is Ra's real name. It was only when he spilt off to form his own group that he started to call himself Ra," explains Cleo.

"Ah, got it," Lauren says. She slides to the floor to get comfier and looks at Cleo. "Your turn," she says in a singsong voice.

Cleo points to herself. "Me? You want my story now?"

Lauren smiles expectantly, and Cleo rolls her eyes good-humoredly. "Well, the quick version," Cleo says, "is that I came into contact with the virus in Colombia as a teenager, but I don't really remember how it happened. Of course now that I have evolved I rarely forget anything, but *that* I don't remember. I will say, the evolution allowed me to survive in an otherwise dangerous part of Colombia. Luckily, Brutus found me, and we left the area in '72, before the American narcos came in and the drug wars further increased violence in the region."

Brutus reaches over and engulfs her hand in his. "It was love at first sight." They smile and exchange glances laden with memories.

"Huh," Lauren says. "Almost everyone's stories seem to line up with the concept that the virus is concentrated at the equator."

Cleo nods.

"The realization that I'm now part of a designated few who have evolved ... that this heightened reality will be my life going forward ... it's blowing my mind a little," Lauren says truthfully. She shakes her head. "But this is Dek's life too, and I need to get him back."

She scrambles up. "Thank you so much, guys, for helping me! I'm going to track down Alexander to see if he has a plan yet."

"No problem, love," says Brutus, putting away another firearm. "Go. We're almost done here, so we'll see you later."

Lauren goes back up to the first floor, finding Frenchy, Maria, and Philippe in the kitchen. Maria is going over some security footage on her computer, and the other two are having some tea.

"Have you guys seen Alexander?" Lauren asks.

"He had to leave for a couple days," Frenchy says. "I think Thi Thi and Carson went with him."

"Yep, I saw them leaving on my security cameras about an hour ago," adds Maria.

"What!" Lauren says, shocked. "What about Dek? We just can't leave him with Ra and the Evos."

"Calm down, my friend," Frenchy says in a comforting voice. "I'm confident Ra will try and convert Decklan before he does anything rash. You see, every convert he gets further reinforces the idea that his beliefs are the correct ones."

"I don't think Dek will convert," Lauren says. "I can't imagine he'd want this ninth evolution to happen."

Maria takes a sip of her tea. "Then they might just bleed him out," she says with a smirk.

"Bleed him out?" Lauren half shrieks. Horrified, she turns to Philippe.

Waving his hands out front in a calming gesture, Philippe says, "She means they will use some of his freshly evolved blood to make Newbies. But I agree with Frenchy; Ra will definitely try and convert him first."

"This is ridiculous!" Lauren exclaims. "There is no time to waste! I know what Ra is looking for. Helms Chemical ... they were procuring the rights to start a mining project in Ecuador. Dek knows the company name but not where. What if the name isn't enough?" She blows out a breath and angrily pushes out the kitchen door.

"I'll check on her." Philippe sets his empty cup in the sink and follows after Lauren. He quickly catches up to her in the upstairs hallway. "Hey wait!" he says. "Wait a second," he repeats, grabbing her arm.

She turns abruptly. "Wait for what?" She yanks her arm free. "For Dek to get bled out?"

Philippe takes a deep breath. "Look, Maria found records that indicate one of Ra's subsidiaries rented a large mansion in North Charleston about two months ago. I can get the address, and you and I can go check it out. Alexander will not be happy with me putting you in harm's way, so let's keep the others in the dark and out of trouble."

She looks at him, stunned, then gives him a big hug. "Thank you, Philippe." Pulling back from the embrace she says, "When do we go?"

CHAPTER 16

Decklan quietly strains against his handcuffs, to no avail. Even focusing all his thoughts on muscle strength does not allow even the slightest movement. It seems Isis was correct. If he could just get free, he could find Lauren and they could find a way out of this together.

He lays his head back on the pillows and lets himself wallow in despair for a few minutes. *What am I thinking? Everyone in this place is evolved, and I have no idea how many there are. I don't know where they are holding Lauren, and it is going to be almost impossible to get the two of us out of here. Not to mention I don't know where* here *is. I'm really getting sick of getting kidnapped and forced into bad situations.*

His train of thought is disrupted as the door opens. A tall, very attractive blond woman comes in and sits in the chair across from his bed. She is wearing a white blouse casually buttoned, black skirt, and blue-rimmed glasses that accent her bright-blue eyes. Her hair is done up in a ponytail dripping down over her left shoulder.

It takes a minute for Dek to recognize her. "Osiris," he says, trying to maintain his calm. "I would say thanks for the drinks, but they gave me quite a hangover."

"Decklan Thomas," she starts, sounding a bit like a lawyer here to offer up a plea deal. "Ra has had his time with you, always trying to find his next convert. I guess now it's my turn. I don't really care if you believe that the ninth evolution is coming or that you are asked to assist us in bringing it to the people of this world. The truth is, it will happen one way or another. You and I and all the other evolved people that you have met should be proof enough that the virus is getting out more and more all on its own. The only thing we are waiting for now is the worldwide release."

"Look, I don't want to talk philosophically with you. I want to see Lauren. I want to talk with her and know that she is okay," he says, trying to take a more forceful stance.

"She is fine," Osiris says, doing the equivalent of crossing her fingers with her emotions to mask her lies. "We will reunite you soon enough. Luckily for you, she has been a lot more helpful in supplying us with the information we need. Now I really only need you to confirm that what she has told us is correct."

"Can't you tell if she is lying?" he asks with a touch of sarcasm.

"She is a very intelligent and resourceful person; she wouldn't be foolish enough to try and boldface lie to me. I just need to hear your truth to see if they match up."

"You won't be getting much from me," he asserts.

She looks at her fingernails, bored. "To be honest, I'm suspicious that you know anything we need at all. Maybe your best use is as a blood donor for the Newbies."

"I've heard all about the things that you are doing. Fooling people into evolving only to watch sixty percent of them die," he says, trying to bluff off her threat.

"Mr. Thomas, you were not given the choice to try for evolution. It was thrust upon you and to your good fortune you have lived and evolved, beat the odds you might say." She uncrosses her legs and leans her elbows on her thighs. "If the choice had been given to you, to evolve and become the person that sits before me, or live on as the person you were for whatever time you have left, what would you choose? Not even taking into account that the ninth happens anyway."

"I have been thinking about that a lot after my conversation with Ra earlier. I think that I would want to live as I did for as long as I could before 'the ninth happens anyway,' as you believe. It's a lot to ask for someone to risk their life with those odds."

"That's what I expected you'd say. You are a healthy White man living in Wisconsin in the richest country in the world." She sneers at his privilege. "What do you think the choice would be for someone a little less fortunate than you? Maybe wanting for a home or clothes or food, or maybe someone who has an illness that would not be a factor if they evolved. Don't you think that person would take a one-in-three chance to live and feel like you do right now?"

Walked right into that one. He turns to humor to deflect his embarrassment. "Well, I really don't feel that great right at this moment, tied to a bed and a captive, but I do see your point."

"Ra is looking out for all these people," she grits out. Her frustration with him is evident. "Yes, some of the less fortunate will die, but the lives of many will be changed for the good. If the world is destroyed before the ninth can occur, then all will be lost. It is our view that bringing on the evolutionary leap before one power-hungry despot kills us all is paramount. The longer the ninth evolution is delayed, the greater the odds that humanity will destroy itself. The timing of these jumps is not only based on when the species is ready to evolve but also based on the fact that the species *must* evolve or risk extinction."

Her logic is so well thought out that Dek feels like he is reeling from physical blows she is meting out. "Okay, again, maybe you have a point, but after it's all over and the whole world has either died or evolved, there is a very good chance that some of these same evil people will remain in power and they will be more powerful than before. All the problems are not necessarily solved."

"You have not been spending enough time with your friend Alexander. Do you think that all of the Children of the Sun are residing here in the Charleston base of operations? Ra and Alexander have lived for over one hundred and fifty years. They have lived through numerous wars, the worst wars in human history. Do you not think that they have been planning for the ninth for decades? There are hundreds of members of the Children and many of them reside in the governments of the most powerful and influential countries of the world. When this goes down—and it will go down—they already have people in place who will take the lead when sixty percent of the others fall. Calm will be restored and the world will go on. The evolutionary jumps are not meant to solve all of the problems of the world. They are to allow our species to continue to develop and survive."

Decklan was feeling good about his own logic until then. He just looks at her, stunned, again caught with his pants down due to a lack of knowledge. "I didn't know that" is all he can muster.

Knowing she's got him on the ropes, Osiris attempts another unexpected move. "Let me put it to you another—"

He quickly interrupts her. "My head is spinning. I'm not sure that I can handle another way right now."

This actually gets her to smile. "Lucky for me, you're a captive audience .... Listen, there are a few identifiable human traits that are essential to our survival as a species. These traits are true in all cultures across the world. Without them, our species would have destroyed itself long ago." She ticks them off on her fingers. "The belief in a higher power or afterlife, desire to reproduce and propagate the species, and need to take over new lands or frontiers—all of these motivators are essential to the development of our species." She pauses and her gaze flickers across his face, wondering if he is buying what she's selling.

He wonders why she stopped. "Please go on, Osiris; the story is just getting good."

She simply glares at him, then calmly continues. "Every culture forms some sort of belief in religion, whether it is forest gods, Greek or Roman gods, Hindu, Christian, or Buddhist gods. The need to believe in a higher power is written into our DNA. The need to reproduce, there is no greater base drive in our makeup. It is not a random chance that most men and women think of sex multiple times a day. Again, across all cultures this is a basic need. Lastly, the need to expand and take over new lands: Every frontier on this planet is gone, except for space and the depths of the oceans. Neither is attainable without the ninth evolution. The evolutionary changes that will result from the ninth evolution will solve all of the problems currently facing this world and this species: hunger, space, pollution, natural resources, disease. It is the only way we survive and move forward."

Dek can't resist and starts clapping dramatically. "Oh my god! You sound like you're giving a graduation speech. If I wasn't literally handcuffed to this bed, I would be standing up right now. You could call that *new frontiers* argument the 'Monopoly effect.' Once all of the properties on the board are purchased and it comes down to building hotels and hopefully draining the other players of their money, the game becomes boring and most people stop. They just count their money to find a winner. The thrill of the game is in obtaining the properties—you nailed it!"

His sarcasm does not go over well if Osiris's chilling look is any indication. She stands, fists clenching and unclenching. "Blood bag it is," she says coldly. She stops with the door held slightly open and talks to the man sitting in the next room. "Could you get him some food and lots of water? We need him to have plenty of blood volume ...."

Dek's head drops heavily onto the pillow. *Time is running out.* He looks down at his handcuffed arm, noticing some bruising and inflammation from straining against the cuffs. He reaches over with his right hand to massage the bruised areas. He quickly notices that the part of his left hand that was cut off and grew back is very pliable. The newly formed bone and tissues haven't fully hardened, kind of like the bones of an infant. He uses his right hand to fold his re-formed fingers toward his thumb. Then, pulling on the cuffs with his right hand, he is able to slide his hand out of the bonds. He takes off a layer of skin in the process, but he is free. Hearing some sounds from outside the room, he repositions the cuffs on his arm so it appears he's still locked up. He still needs some information before he can make his escape.

CHAPTER 17

The door opens again. This time, it's the man who was guarding his room. He comes in with a tray of food and a large jug, presumably full of water. He puts the tray down on the table. Dek can hear his cells buzzing. *He must be a Newbie*, Dek thinks, *yet to be fully trained at hiding this sound, and maybe at hiding a lie ....*

"Hey, buddy," Dek says, drawing his attention. "I know that you chose to go down this path because you believe in Ra. My girlfriend and I are not here of our free will. Can you at least tell me if she's okay?" he asks, paying very close attention to the guard's response.

The man straightens up, not expecting a conversation. "I'm not supposed to talk to you," he says coldly.

"Come on," Dek pleads, "I just want to know if she's okay."

He stares at Dek, clearly mulling it over in his head. "She is doing fine."

"Thanks, that means a lot," Dek responds, taking a sip of water.

When the guard turns to walk out, Dek leaps up and smacks him in the back of the head with the water jug. The man slumps to the floor.

"Sorry, dude, but I have other plans for this evening, and you just let me know that Lauren is not here. They must not have been able to get us both," Dek says to himself, locking the guy's arm to the cuffs on the bed and checking the door.

He slowly opens the door, ready for an attack, but the area is empty. There is a desk and a monitoring screen with an image of his room on one side and an outer door on the other. Dek finds a pistol in one of the drawers and a syringe filled with something, maybe a sedative. He takes them both and listens at the other door. After a few seconds of silence, Dek cracks the second door. He can see a window at the end of the short hallway. It's night, but a tree is clearly visible on the left. *I should be able to climb down that and get outta here.*

Dek begins creeping down the hallway and notices another door just past the window. He listens at the door and can hear what he believes is someone gaming. He cracks the door and sees a man with headphones on, deeply immersed in a video game. He sneaks up behind the man, covers the guy's mouth, and shoots the syringe into the side of his neck. After a few seconds of struggle the man's head lolls to the side.

Seeing that the coast is clear, Dek opens the window and removes the screen. He lowers himself onto a tree branch, then swiftly makes his way down to the ground. Quickly looking around, Dek sees that the front of the house is lit up pretty well, but the side only has some low-level landscape lighting. He guesses he has to make it across about fifty feet of open ground to make it to the tree line and fence. From there he can try and find a main road before his captors discover he's gone.

Dek takes off across the grass and, in seconds using his amped-up speed, leaps over the fence. He hears a soft beeping sound and sees a motion sensor positioned just outside the fence, flashing a small red light. Suddenly the floodlights attached to the house are ablaze and he can hear the animated voices of the men in the house. Dek starts tearing through the woods as fast as his legs can go, branches scratching his arms and face. Headlights are coming right at him from about thirty yards ahead. He pops out of the woods and starts frantically waving his arms to get the car's attention. Too late he realizes that the car was already slowing down as it approached the house's main driveway entrance. *This must be one of the Evos returning.* He diverts and turns back toward the woods, heading away from the house.

"Dek! Dek!" Lauren yells from the car, popping open the passenger side door as the car screeches to a halt. "Oh my god! Get in!"

Dek runs over and dives into the back seat. "Go! Go now!"

Philippe spins the wheel and guns the engine, heading back in the direction they were coming from. He turns off the car lights and uses his enhanced vision to navigate the darkness. He sees the headlights of two trucks pulling out of the driveway behind them in the distance, but both seem to be shining lights into the woods and not trying to pursue them as they round a bend, out of eyesight of the trucks.

Lauren turns around as Dek leans forward between the front seats. She wraps her arms around his neck, squeezing him so hard he feels the breath get knocked out of him.

"Easy, beautiful. Superstrength, remember?" Dek squeaks out before she lets him go. "I can't believe you guys are here," he adds as he sits back in relief.

"We were coming to rescue you," Lauren says, starting to talk a mile a minute. "And I guess we did. I was so scared that this was going to be a complete shit show, that we could get hurt or have to hurt someone else. Oh my god, what a relief."

"The timing couldn't have been better," confirms Philippe. "How did you manage to get out?"

"It was something out of a movie," he starts, before telling them about his harrowing escape.

"What did they want from you?" asks Lauren.

"I'm not one hundred percent sure. I mainly talked with Ra and Osiris. It seemed more like recruitment than interrogation .... I think they were going to use me for the virus in my blood."

"Well, I'm so glad to have you back," Lauren says, reaching her hand back to squeeze Dek's hand one more time.

**

Five minutes earlier in a downstairs meeting room, Ra, Isis, Osiris, and Anubis are sitting around a large circular table.

"He is showing too much resistance to the recruitment tactics," Osiris says, drumming her fingers on the table impatiently. "I think we should drain him for a while, drug him, and interrogate him. I'm not into wasting any more time."

"The matter of his usefulness beyond a blood donor has been settled via another route," drawls Ra, not bothering to look up from his laptop. "Helms Chemical is the company we're looking for. I am scanning its project dossier as we speak." He hums to himself as his fingers fly over the keyboard. "Okay, not on their primary project list ... must be something that they are keeping hush hush." He continues to type away, and the others sit silently, exchanging we've-been-here-before looks.

"All right, I think I got it," Ra says triumphantly. "They have a project in Ecuador under a subcompany that's supposedly looking for botanical ingredients in the jungle. Nope. That's a ruse. Look at this." He turns the laptop around so everyone can see. "The amount of heavy equipment and manpower listed for the project can only be a mining site. Since the materials that were being tested by Decklan and Lauren had viral-containing dirt on them, I would assume they were testing technetium. Its radiation signature keeps the virus dormant. It makes sense that Helms Chemical must have found a source of naturally occurring technetium, and they are preparing to mine it in Ecuador. What would a chemical company want with that? I have no idea," he finishes, talking to himself.

The laptop suddenly starts flashing red, and the outside floodlights come blazing to life.

"What now?" says Anubis, getting up and peering out a front-facing window.

Ra, unfazed, turns the laptop back around and begins typing. "It seems our new friend didn't like the idea of being a viral donor .... His value to us is greatly diminished, but if one of you wants to go after him, be my guest. We could always use an evolved blood source."

"Bloody hell," Anubis says and pulls out his cell phone. "I'll send some guys out with spotlights. If they find him, great. If the little piggy wants to run all the way home, I don't think it's worth the hassle."

Ra draws everyone's attention back with a few loud raps on the table. Pointing to his computer, he says, "This is the information we have been waiting for! Osiris, I want you to scout the site and put together a plan of action. If we are confident that the dig site is looking for what we think they are, we could be starting the ninth evolution as soon as next month."

Osiris looks up from her phone. "I started looking for flights as soon as you said 'Ecuador.' I'm leaving at nine a.m. tomorrow."

CHAPTER 18

It only takes a half hour for Philippe to get them back within the protective confines of the compound. It takes slightly longer for them to get through the lecture Alexander gives them for attempting a rescue mission without the support of everyone on the team.

"We were working on a plan to get him out with less risk," Alexander admonishes. He drones on, at least crediting them on some level for their success, before talk turns to dissecting the events.

"The level of pursuit was odd, like almost nonexistent," Philippe says thoughtfully, scratching his chin. "If they went through all that trouble to get Dek, why let him escape so easily? Unless they got what they needed from him."

"True. What did Ra question you about while you were there?" asks Alexander.

"It seemed more like a get-to-know-you recruitment interview," replies Dek with a slight shrug. "They actually did a lot of the talking. In fact, I don't think they ever asked me anything that would be useful to them." He pauses and with a huge grin regales them with his mockery of Osiris. "She was definitely annoyed that I wasn't on board with Ra's plans—like, literally ready to have me drained for my blood's viral load after our conversation." He winks at Lauren.

"On that level, I can sympathize with her," says Lauren, cracking a grin and giving him a squeeze on the arm.

Alexander crosses his legs and lightly taps his thumb on his knee. "It is possible Dek unknowingly let something slip that proved helpful to them. It's also possible they got the information they needed from another source, which would make more sense with the lackluster response to his escape—especially if Dek wasn't responsive to their recruitment propaganda. Okay, so let's presume they are moving forward with whatever they found out." He turns to Philippe. "I want you at the Charleston airport looking for any of our friends trying to leave the area. Find out where they're going. Based on Lauren's intel, have Maria start digging into this Helms Chemical. Maybe we can figure out Ra's plans if we have more information."

"I'll go now and talk to Maria on my way out," says Philippe, heading for the door.

"As for you two, it's been a rough couple of days," Alexander says, opening a new page on his laptop. "Maybe a little rest would be in order?"

Dek nods. "It's been nonstop insanity since we had the accident. I think I need a vacation, not just a nap." He holds the door for Lauren. "We'll see you tomorrow."

They trudge to their room in relative silence, but their relief at being reunited and safe, at least for the time being, is palpable. Lauren catches a quick glimpse of the garden through the window and sees Thi Thi sitting at a table. "Hey, Dek, give me a few minutes and I'll meet you back at the room," she says, patting his shoulder.

Lauren slowly walks into the garden, feeling a bit intimidated.

"Don't be shy," Thi Thi says and waves her over.

"Hey, Thi Thi." Lauren sits gingerly in the seat across from her. "Um, so Philippe mentioned that you are the true master of the group when it comes to hand-to-hand fighting ... and I, uh, really want to get better at that."

Thi Thi's mouth turns up slightly. "That boy is quick, but still no match for my experience." She feigns an awkward karate chop, and Lauren laughs. The older woman nods at her. "Yes, of course. If we have time, young one, I'd be happy to train you."

Lauren basks in the older woman's warmth. She sits back in her chair and crosses her ankles. "When *did* you evolve?"

Thi Thi shrugs it off. "In the early 1920s, when I was sixteen … not really sure how it happened, but it quickly changed the course of my life."

"I bet!" Lauren says. "I'm feeling exactly that about my own life right now …. So how did you come to the group?" She side-eyes the older woman and adds, "Kidnapped, perchance?"

Thi Thi smirks. "No. Victor actually heard of my growing prowess and guessed accurately that I was evolved. After witnessing me kill two men in a ring fight, though, he returned to Alexander and told him that I was too violent and out of control for the group they were starting to form."

"I can imagine being a female fighter would cause a lot of insecure men to challenge you," Lauren says softly.

"I had sharpened, poison-tipped fingernails that I used my evolution to harden like those of the lion. Not one warrior could take me down," she says, stretching out her fingers toward Lauren.

Lauren raises an eyebrow at that image.

"But, despite Ra's reluctance, Alexander chose to see for himself. He was adamant that all evolved people support each other. Upon arriving at my small village, Alexander told me of a rival tribal leader's plan to kill me. They believed that my superior combat skills were the work of the devil. Alexander wanted me to leave with him and learn to harness my gifts for good, but I was headstrong and stubborn and I rejected his offer. Later that night I found his camp and killed the two unevolved men that were traveling with him. I squared off against Alexander, claws dripping with the blood of his friends. His cells started to hum louder and louder, soon causing terrible pain in my own evolved—yet untrained—ears. I ran from the fight holding my ears in agony."

"Wow, I have heard some pretty loud-sounding cells," Lauren says, thinking back to her first sighting of Frenchy in Chicago. "But I can't imagine it getting that loud."

"It is one of Alexander's gifts, highly effective against a Newbie. I returned to my village, raging with anger over my defeat. I immediately went to the village whose leader had plans to kill me, and I murdered his entire family."

Lauren gasps.

Thi Thi slowly nods her head, remorse and shame written all over her face.

"In the next week, all of the surrounding villages banded together and attacked our village. Everyone was killed. I alone remained, badly injured, making a last stand against at least ten warriors. Alexander returned with a small group of men with rifles. The villagers ran, and Alexander took me back to Cairo. He helped me to heal my injuries and allowed me to be educated in more than just dominance and warfare. I truly felt indebted to him, though he never claimed that to be the case. I still stand by him today, as a friend, and maybe in some ways a protector."

"I just got goose bumps," Lauren says, rubbing her arms.

Thi Thi smiles wanly. "That is not a story I enjoy recalling, but I hope you learn something from it." She stands. "We will talk again soon and find time to train."

"Thanks so much, Thi Thi. Have a good night."

***

Dek closes the bedroom door softly behind Lauren.

She wraps him in a giant hug, burying her head in his chest, and he follows suit, surrounding her with a protective squeeze.

"I really missed you," he whispers into her hair.

She gives him a squeeze.

"Easy on the hugs, or I might have cracked ribs to heal," he wheezes.

She lets up and moves in to give him a long, deep kiss.

"Wow," he says, coming up for air. He holds her chin firmly with one hand, looking into her eyes. "I can't believe how much I missed you. Even the sound of your cells is a comfort to me."

"Show me," she says with a mischievous smile.

So he does.

Hours later, completely sated, they fall into a deep and rewarding slumber.

***

The sun is peeking through the cracks in the blinds when Decklan rolls over onto his back. Lauren gets up on one elbow, squinting at the bright light, then flops back, scooting to rest her head on his chest.

"If that's the kind of welcome back I get, I might have to get kidnapped more often," Dek says, his voice still gruff with sleep.

"If we can just manage *not* to get kidnapped again, I'll be happy to give you as many nights like that as you can handle," she says, nestling into him.

"I'm going to hold you to that," he says with a kiss to her forehead. "But we're not having a lot of success in the not-getting-kidnapped area lately, so who knows?"

Lauren laughs and gets out of bed. She walks to the window and rolls up the shade. Dek can barely see the outline of her shadowed naked body in the bright sunlight. "You better get back into bed; you're putting on a show at the window," he informs her.

She poses demurely and then waves him off. "Believe it or not, I need a shower," she quips and proceeds to the bathroom.

Dek can't manage to remove the smile from his face as he recalls their night together. He yawns loudly and rolls back over in bed to hug the pillow Lauren slept on. He inhales deeply, fully enjoying the combination of smells—her perfume, her shampoo, the smell of her skin still lingering in the sheets. Even though this has been one of the craziest periods of his life, having Lauren here to go through it with gives him hope for the future. Truthfully, he can finally see a future forming in front of him. Every moment that he spends with her is better than the last, even the tough ones. He sits up on the side of the bed, stretching and waking up his body. *Wherever this crazy ride takes us*, he thinks, *I see a future worth fighting for.*

After a few more minutes, Lauren emerges in her workout gear, pulling her hair into a ponytail. "You know, you have a lot of catching up to do," she taunts him with a grin. "While you were gone, Philippe showed me some new fighting techniques, and Brutus and Cleo took me to the gun range. You won't be able to keep up with me!"

"We'll see about that," he says, slapping her ass on his way to the bathroom. "Let me get a shower and I'll meet you downstairs."

"Okay, I'll see you down there," she says and, with a flip of her ponytail, walks out the door.

Chapter 19

A cup of coffee, a plate of fresh fruit, and a Danish pastry await Dek on the kitchen island. He can hear a hum of conversation pouring in through the patio door. He adds the appropriate, or maybe slightly excessive, amount of creamer to his cup and heads out into the bright sunshine. Alexander is seated at the head of a large wrought iron table just beyond the patio covering with Thi Thi at his side. Next is Lauren, with an empty seat beside her. Brutus's huge body takes up the end opposite Alexander, along with Cleo and Carson. Urvinder and Frenchy are sitting at a smaller table about twenty feet away, having a quieter conversation in what looks like a quaint tea party.

Frenchy immediately gets up when he sees Dek elbow the door open. "Ah good, I see you have found the plate we left out for you." He gestures to the chair next to Lauren. "We have saved you a seat at the children's table. Please try and be good," he says with a smile.

Dek is greeted with a series of "good mornings" as he takes his seat. Casually nudging Lauren's arm before digging into his plate, he asks, "What have I missed?"

"Aside from a few less-than-PG jokes, not a whole lot," says Brutus, laughing. His heavy voice just booms even in the open air of the gardens.

"We do have some news," says Alexander, taking the lead. "Maria has done some research on Helms Chemical, and it does seem that they are most likely Ra's next target and strongest chance to release his ninth evolution. They have a large excavation and mining site that they recently greenlighted in Ecuador. It's very likely that this area is the originating site of the viral samples that infected Decklan and Lauren. Maria was able to forward her findings to Philippe, who is watching the airports. If any of the Evos crew are on a flight bound for Ecuador, we can assume that is their target and that they let Dek go because they got that information from another source."

"Both of those confirmations will be significant in what we do going forward," interjects Thi Thi. "If the Evos are going to Ecuador to cause the evolution, then we, too, must go to stop them. If they gained this information from another source, then it is safe to assume that it could have come from someone here who is leaking information to Ra."

They all turn quiet, even causing Dek to stop chewing due to the sound becoming magnified by the silence.

Alexander raises his hands in a calming gesture. "We were once one big family, then divided by how the evolution will come to be. We all had friends on that other side …. Maybe some of us are still friends with the people who share this different view?" He sighs, and his gaze flickers over them all. "So, to prevent our intentions from being leaked to Ra and potentially putting one of our team in danger, you will be receiving your assignments individually and discreetly. You all should have a good idea of what may be required of you; be prepared to do that and to move out at any time. Decklan and Lauren, your limited training and experience could make you more of a liability than an advantage. I will assess how to best use you when the need arises."

Dek and Lauren nod, and everyone else remains quiet.

Alexander slaps his hands on his knees. "Good. Thi Thi and I have some preparations to attend to. I will let you know when I have more information."

The team watches them for a few moments as they walk along the stone path through the garden to their side of the compound. Lauren is the first to speak. "Dek and I do not want to be benched due to lack of experience. Are any of you training today? I had a good go of it this week, and it was very helpful. If we could get Dek some of that same training, I think we would both feel a lot better about what's to come."

"Yeah, love, Cleo and I are always a go for lighting up the range," Brutus says candidly. "Meet you down there in half an hour or so?" He looks at Cleo for confirmation and she nods. "We'll probably be packing up the lot when we're done to be ready to go, so I highly recommend any of you who want a brushup to get down there today."

Carson, who was helping Frenchy clear the food and drinks, hoists the heavy tray and makes his way to the door behind Brutus and Cleo. "I can show you some strength and hand-to-hand training later this afternoon if you like," he offers.

As silence once again fills the patio, Dek leans his head back, the palms of his hands over his eyes. "Do you think we're ready for this?" he asks Lauren wearily.

The light tapping sound of a cane on cobblestones suddenly draws their attention, reminding them that Urvinder is still there.

Dek hops up and pulls out a chair for her. "Hey, Urvinder, would you like to join us?"

Urvinder eases down into the seat next to Lauren.

"How has your morning been?" Lauren asks pleasantly.

"Good. The sun is out, the gardens are beautiful, everything is good .... Well, except for maybe the news," Urvinder replies frankly.

"I think, uh, we're a bit worried about the news as well," says Lauren. "What do *you* think will happen?"

"Victor will force the evolution," Urvinder states rather matter-of-factly. "He is laser focused on this goal, and he will do everything he can to make it happen."

Dek nods. "Ra told me he was afraid that if he waited too long, mankind would destroy itself."

Urvinder seems lost in thought as she taps her cane on the ground. "Over the last hundred and twenty years, he has lost faith in the ability of the unevolved to make decisions for the good of all, not just for the good of themselves," she says morosely.

A heavy silence briefly fills the air.

"Forgive me for changing the subject, but I was wondering something .... Urvinder Gurm is an Indian name, is it not? But you look more like someone of Central African descent," Dek says.

Urvinder squints over at him. "That is an astute observation, Mr. Thomas. As you know, I don't age like regular people. In order to maintain my existence in society, I've had to assume new identities every fifty years to avoid detection. The last time I did so was while I was a housemaid for an Indian couple in a small town in southern Pennsylvania." She pauses briefly and closes her eyes, breathing in the sun. "They had a child who passed in the 1900s, and allowed me to use the birth certificate and other documents to assume this final identity. My evolved adaptations allowed me to quickly become fluent with their language and customs. I could even change the pigmentation of my skin if I ran into any staunch disbelievers."

Lauren inhales sharply. "Final identity?" she asks quietly. "Do you not think we will survive the coming conflict?"

"Dear, I am closing in on two hundred years old," Urvinder says, softly patting Lauren's hand. "We cannot keep our cells fresh forever, and my time is approaching. Hopefully, I can use the time I have left to help this world in one final way."

They hear the somber note in her voice. Lauren squeezes the older woman's hand gently, then shoots a look at Dek as if to say, *Should I do it?* He nods resolutely. Both have been dying to ask the question since their arrival.

"So, er, Urvinder, ..." Lauren begins shyly, "no one seems to know how you froze me and Dek—or, um, so effectively neutralized us without actually harming either of us. Is that something you can teach us?"

Urvinder places her hands in her lap and looks down at them for a moment. "That is a question that I have been asked by almost every member of the Children of the Sun," she says with a sigh. "My usual reply is no, and I move on. The truth is, I am not sure precisely how I do it, but it came to me through a life-or-death situation …. This is not a pretty story, but I will tell it if you like?" She looks at Dek and Lauren, who nod solemnly.

"Just after the Civil War, I was working in the fields on a plantation outside of Charleston. You should know that the conditions didn't get much better immediately after slavery was ended. The men running the plantations were angry and often took that out on the workers. There were new laws, but they were rarely enforced, especially against the wealthy landowners ….

"Anyway," she says with a wave of her hand, "the plantation I worked for hired an ex–Confederate soldier to oversee our work crew. He was a giant of a man, almost the size of Brutus. One day, he came up behind me—his heartbeat was calm, so I didn't sense any danger from him—and I turned to say hello. My confidence, or arrogance, that in my evolved state I could handle anything this man could say or do to me was a grave miscalculation. He punched me in the side of the head without saying a word. I dropped to my knees, stunned by the blow. He grabbed my hair and shoved my face into the muddy soil. My first attempt at breath just sucked in mud. I was in a full panic mode as he tore at my clothes. My heart raced and my mind screamed. Then he just stopped. His grip on my hair released, and I yanked free, gasping for air. I scrambled away and cleared the mud from my eyes. He was just frozen there, kneeling down on one leg with his penis out, his eyes staring at me in fear. I could feel a connection to the cells of his body, and I somehow knew that *I* was why he could not move."

"I am so sorry that happened to you," says Lauren tearfully. "What happened to him?"

Urvinder clears her throat. "I used his own knife to cut the artery on his leg. I stood and watched him bleed out. Eventually the light left his eyes, and he collapsed forward into the very mud that he tried to drown me in." She peered into Lauren's eyes, then Decklan's. "You should know that I do not regret killing that man …. Since then, I learned that I could think back to that moment and invoke this panic response, basically stunning someone's cells. I worked for many years honing that skill, but I could never teach another how to do it."

"So every time you 'freeze' someone, you have to think back to that moment?" Lauren asks, aghast. "That's just horrible."

Before Urvinder can answer, the door bursts open, startling them all.

"All right, mates, enough lazing around. Let's get down to the range and shoot some shit up," Brutus booms from the doorway.

The three at the table exchange looks, and Brutus raises his hands in a questioning gesture, feeling as if he just interrupted something. Then Urvinder hoots. Her infectious laughter causes Dek and Lauren to crack up as well.

"That's one way to lighten the mood," Urvinder says, wiping her eyes.

CHAPTER 20

Mr. Helms is sitting at the head of a long conference table, gazing out the bank of windows lining the far wall at the city of Quito. Feldman knocks briefly before entering. He is followed by a young woman with a pitcher of water and tray of glasses. She sets them down and promptly leaves.

"Is she here yet?" asks Helms, still staring out the window.

"I believe she will be arriving shortly," replies Feldman, taking a seat next to Helms and placing his workbag on the table.

"I never would have agreed to this meeting if not for her interest in technetium. All the contracts and permits filed with the Ecuadorean government indicated our interest in cosmetics-related products ... so how did she even know that was what we are doing here?" Helms asks, swiveling around to face Feldman.

"She is under the belief that we are looking for something else in our digs but discovered that technetium could be near the areas we are mining," Feldman says. "She claims her company would like to piggyback off our mining project."

"I think it's all bullshit," Helms scoffs, "but let's find out what she's really after and, frankly, how she even found out that we were here."

The phone in Feldman's jacket pocket starts to buzz. He glances down at the screen. "She is in the waiting room. I'll go down now and get her."

Feldman returns and appears a little frazzled as he holds the door open for a tall, blond-haired woman wearing a gray business suit and black heels. The woman exudes confidence as she greets Helms.

"Hello, I'm Olivia Osiris," she says, shaking his hand. "I represent the interests of Pinnacle Rock and Gemstone. We specialize in the acquisition of rare ore and gems." She slides her small black purse off her shoulder and hangs it on the chair next to Helms, then places her briefcase on the floor before taking a seat.

"We were rather surprised when you contacted us," Helms admits. "Just out of curiosity, how did you find out that we're here?"

Osiris smiles and crosses her legs. "We monitor mining permits and have several, say, connections in the areas that we have mining interests," she says nonchalantly. "We were made aware months ago when your initial survey team got themselves killed in Colombia."

"An unfortunate event that did have some press coverage," Helms mumbles, pouring himself a glass of water.

"We have interest in technetium, which we believe may be available at deeper dig levels at the site you are working at. It is highly radioactive and requires special permits for removal." She pauses to lift her briefcase to the table. "You have not procured these permits; therefore, we believe that your interest here is in something in the upper crust levels."

Helms eyes her coolly. *She keeps boxing with me. Technetium is almost the only thing of worth that we could possibly be seeking here, and she knows we didn't get the permits yet to go after it legally.*

"We have agreements with the Ecuadorean government with regard to *whatever* it is that we are looking for," he fires back cryptically.

She places some paperwork in front of her and smoothly turns it so Helms can read the text. "We could have the permits and a sizable financing package if you were to change your mind and want to dig deeper," she tells him.

Helms glances down briefly at the papers, then takes another drink of water. She simply stares at him. They are both trying hard to get a read on each other. Osiris is having a very difficult time telling if he is lying. He's either very practiced at it, or he is telling the truth.

"I will have my lawyers look over your proposal and get back to you, but I wouldn't hold my breath," he tells her. He knows he just has to bide his time. They are so far along, they'd have what they need in just a couple of days.

She nods and slowly raps her fingernails on the table. "I was hoping to tour the dig site while I'm here," she casually says, hoping to pick up some more intel and make it easier for Ra to develop his plans.

"No," Helms responds bluntly. "Ours is a closed site. I can't have any competitors snooping around."

She nods slowly. "That's understandable," she says. Standing up, she offers Helms her hand once more. "I will leave you with our proposal, then. I'm staying at the Hilton, if you need to get hold of me."

Feldman smiles pathetically at her. "If you would like some company for dinner or someone to see the city with, you have my card," he whispers and watches her walk down the hallway.

"Get over here, you idiot," Helms scolds him.

Feldman blinks rapidly. "I don't know what came over me," he stammers. "She is just breathtaking."

"Her hormone levels are off the charts. It will be a miracle if she can walk down the street without a trail of men following behind her," Helms says, picking up the proposal that she left for him. "Double the privacy guards at the site. I don't think she is a woman who is used to men saying no to her."

Feldman nods and pulls out his phone, then pauses to read an incoming text. "It's the Heretic Group," he tells Helms, then reads the message aloud. "*We have identified three men who worked with the men who drove the explosive truck into the dig site. We are holding them in the bunkhouse at the camp."*

"Finally some good news," says Helms, leaning back and swiveling his chair.

"What do you want done with them?" Feldman asks.

Helms smiles. "What do you think? Should we kill them to send a message or ship them off?"

Feldman walks to the window while he ponders the question. "Killing them would definitely send a message to the other workers, but sending them away may accomplish the same task without angering the surrounding villages that have been the main source of our workforce." He turns back to Helms. "Sending them away shows that we are able to identify who is working against us yet are willing to show mercy for loyalty going forward."

"Okay, I'll go along with that line of thought. But if the locals step out of line again, we kill them and then bring these fuckers back and kill them too," Helms says coldly.

***

As the elevator doors close, Osiris easily shuts down the hormone array she was emitting. She puts her hair up in a pony and puts on her fashion eyeglasses, but still emerges looking like a model. Her hotel is just a few blocks down from the offices, and she pulls out her phone on the walk, dialing Ra.

She gives him the quick rundown and scoffs when Ra says, "I'm impressed that an unevolved person was not influenced by your charms." He thinks for a moment. "Well, I was hoping for easy access, but I'll just have to send the full team over in the next few weeks."

"I would send them into the airport in Tulcan," Osiris suggests. "It seems like Helms has this Quito airport under surveillance. And I actually flew out of Charlotte in case Alexander's crew was casing the Charleston airport. While I don't really expect much in the way of resistance from a chemical company, there is no need to tip our hand."

"Smart moves. I can do that," he says, typing away on his laptop. "I may even send Anubis and Isis in through Colombia." He pauses to rub his eyes. "And I agree, the Helms Chemical crew are probably the least of our concerns."

She laughs. "With their reckless way of doing things, they might have the dig site blown up before we even get our plan together."

"They do seem rather amateurish, don't they," Ra agrees. "If Alexander is sending in the Children of the Sun to counter our efforts, that will be our biggest challenge. But I have some ideas to keep them occupied here until it is done. In the meantime, I'll get the satellite imagery of the site forwarded to you to help with the planning. We may need to acquire a warehouse or staging site to organize our equipment. See what intel you can gather there in town."

"I'll see what I can do," Osiris assures him. As she is about to pocket her phone, it begins to buzz. *Now there's a number that I haven't seen in a while*, she thinks, pausing for a second before answering.

"Hello, my love, how can I help you?" she answers with a note of indifference.

"I think we need to meet," says the voice on the other end.

"I am currently out of the country. Any desires to rekindle will have to wait until I return."

"This is important!"

Her phone buzzes as another call is coming in. She recognizes the number that Helms's assistant used to talk with her earlier. She decides not to answer; let him stew for a while. *My charms are working just fine*, she thinks.

"I'm afraid that I have another call; we will have to catch up later," she says, hanging up the line. She takes a deep breath. *The pieces are starting to fall into place.*

CHAPTER 21

"**B**ob Seger sang about 'echoes of amplifiers ringing in your head'? Well, I've got echoes of gunfire!" Dek says to Lauren—very loudly—after a few hours in the gun range.

Lauren winces. "I should have warned you," she says, putting a gentle hand on his shoulder as they walk to their room. "With our advanced hearing, even with ear protection it's pretty harsh on your ears."

"I don't think I've ever shot off that many rounds before," Dek says. "But I really did learn a ton. My evolved sight gives me the accuracy of a scope without the need of the piece of equipment."

"If you can make out everything Bru is saying through that heavy Aussie accent, he gives lots of great instruction."

"C'mon now, don't shoot like a limp-wristed sheila. What kinda bloke are you?" Dek thunders, playfully trying to mimic Brutus.

They get to the top of the stairs and turn into the hallway, almost running into Frenchy, who is swiftly walking back from knocking on their door.

"Oh! There you are, my friends," he says excitedly. "Do you think I could have a word?"

"Sure, Frenchy," says Lauren.

"Meet me on the upper terrace in ten? I'll run down and grab us a bite to munch on while we talk."

"Yeah, no problem," Dek confirms, looking at Lauren for an okay. "I would love something to eat. I'm starving."

"Great, I'll see you there in a few," Frenchy says and proceeds down to the kitchen.

Decklan closes the door to their room. "That guy takes really great care of us, like five-star service."

"He does, but ... I'm not sure how I feel about the way he uses the 'my friends' line so much," says Lauren, freshening up in the bathroom. "He reminds me of the employees on a cruise ship who always say the same line to each new passenger. 'My friend. Hello, sir.' Washy washy. They use the same phrases over and over to sound nice and generic."

Dek sits on the bed, waiting his turn at the sink. "Are you saying he's being fake? I remember Alexander saying Frenchy used to work for a hotel ... maybe that's what you're picking up on?"

"I don't know if 'fake' is the right term; just feels a little slick, ya know?" she says, walking into the room. "I'm pretty sure the people working on the cruise have very different opinions in private of the people that they 'my friend' to in the open."

Dek sidles over and grabs Lauren by the hips to gently pull her closer. She smiles up at him. "Honestly, Frenchy's been nothing but wonderful; I'm just trying to keep my guard up around all of them," she admits.

He leans in for a kiss, and she turns, giving him cheek. "Evolved taste and smell, buddy. The toothbrush is in there, then you can kiss me out here," she says playfully, pushing away from him.

He smiles. "Be right back."

A few minutes later, Dek and Lauren have to force themselves to leave the room.

***

Frenchy pushes through the door backward, balancing a tray of food and drinks. Dek jumps up from his seat, helping with the door and removing a bottle of wine from the tray. Frenchy sets the tray down on the table and straightens out any of the food that shifted as he came out. Dek goes to the minibar and gets a wine opener for a rather large bottle of pinot grigio.

"There are some chilled glasses in the freezer to the left," Frenchy calls over to Dek.

They finally all settle down around the table, each with a glass of wine and a small plate of food.

"So what's up?" asks Lauren, enjoying a sip of wine.

"Well, my friends, I am very concerned about the potential conflict that we may be facing in the coming days. I have lived through many years of war in my lifetime, and I fear the loss of good friends that I have on both sides. I guess ... my true questions are for Decklan, having recently been the guest of Ra."

Dek and Lauren exchange surprised glances.

"No problem, what did you want to know?" Dek replies.

"Did you actually get to talk with Victor much or were you more of a prisoner?" Frenchy starts.

"I did speak with Ra. He gave me more of a join-our-group pitch than an interrogation. Later I got a one-on-one with Osiris, the woman who drugged us," he adds for Lauren. "But she really had a lot of the same. I didn't tell them anything about you guys here, though. I really don't know much to tell them."

"Oh, I'm not asking to accuse you of anything," Frenchy quickly clarifies. "I'm hoping you're going to tell me his obsession with the ninth evolution has cooled ...." He sighs. "You see, Victor and I were very close for many years. Did you know that I worked with him on his evolutionary timeline? Many, many years of research, theory, and discovery—some of the best years of my life. So I'm trying to figure out if there is a chance of negotiating with him to avoid the looming conflict."

"I did *not* get the impression that his passion has flagged. At all. But maybe if you were able to speak with him ..." Dek replies, trailing off.

Frenchy takes a sip of wine and stares off over the harbor.

"You never know, if you had a chance to talk, what might be accomplished," adds Lauren hopefully.

"On second thought," Dek says, pointing his mini-sandwich at Frenchy, "I don't think I would risk it if I were you. If Ra is this dead set on bringing about the ninth evolution, he could use you as a way to stop Alexander from stopping him."

Frenchy nods slowly and rubs his chin while thinking, then smiles reluctantly toward Dek in acknowledgment. "Part of the research that we did was to look at threats to the species or the planet which would potentially stop the evolution. It seemed to us that these leaps were set up not only for when the species was ready to move forward but also for when the planet needed it to move forward. He is also looking at the population density, the pollution causing changes in the climates and weather, the lack of water and natural resources needed to support the current population," Frenchy explains.

"Ra is looking at the casualties of the evolution as a necessary part of the evolution. A resetting of the resources needed to maintain the species and protect the planet. So when you were mapping the timeline, Ra was looking for things that could be obstacles to the next evolution?" Dek asks.

"He believes that the new human will be able to understand what is needed to run the planet right. The enhanced ability to think, learn, and understand will not be limited to the few who can afford it. Education is one of the biggest obstacles to stopping violence, unchecked breeding, hate, bigotry, and racism. Which are all modern plagues on our species. All people will suddenly be on an even playing field as far as education goes, and resources will be in abundance so that they can be shared without threat of them being used up. Ra doesn't want something to happen before the evolution that would not allow the evolution to occur. So he'll make it occur himself."

"Look, Frenchy, you don't have to sell us on the good that would potentially be achieved. It's the cost of all those innocent lives. It's one thing to say that this happened and now we have to live with it. It's quite another to say that we brought it about because we decided what was best for everyone," says Lauren.

"It's a lot easier for him to say let's go ahead and cause this now because he already knows that he is one of the ones who gets to live. He knows he's not going to die but wants to make the call, to roll the dice for everyone else. That's what I have a problem with," adds Dek. "Tell people the odds and let the world decide."

"He's afraid that that information would be the exact thing that could cause a global panic and actually cause the powers of the world to destroy it. Just imagine, you would have a cataclysmic world on fire, as people feared or hoped for something that they have no control over."

Dek just shakes his head. "It is a very complex topic. I see people today absolutely losing it over the littlest things. I can't imagine what kind of crisis information like this could cause."

"Not meaning to shift the conversation, but you said that you worked with Ra in the development of his evolutionary timeline. How did you come up with the dates? Could he be wrong in thinking that the ninth evolution is coming soon?" asks Lauren.

"We went over it at least a thousand times, my friends. I wish that it was that simple, to say the dates were wrong. Because of the ambiguity of pi, Ra just needs to believe that he is in the ballpark to justify his actions. We started about six million years ago when the molecular evidence presented in genes and proteins showed a jump from chimps to the human species evolutionary line. There are points in time where the species jumps forward evolutionarily but still remains uniform. An example of this is two chimps living in the same jungle in Africa might have greater species differences than anyone along the human line. Archeological evidence shows how the human species advanced in skull or brain size and the ability to use tools and make shelters. Along this path we also have various subspecies that died off and weren't part of the current line. Using the evidence that we could find, we could see a timeline forming that showed the evolutionary leaps were happening at an increasing rate or at a decreasing time interval between jumps. In other words, the speed at which we have advanced as a species over the last one hundred years is far greater than it was two million years ago."

"And you found that these jumps were roughly occurring at a decreasing time frequency related to pi?" confirms Dek.

"Again, this was determined to the best of our ability with the information that we had available. We were also looking at the many environmental and sociologic signs that it is time for our species to move forward. It all points to the ninth evolution occurring *soon*." Frenchy confirms, making air quotes with his fingers.

"Not to mention us," says Lauren. "The fact that we have evolved due to a tiny release of the virus indicates that man has the ability to release the virus, rather than it happening only due to a natural disaster or accident."

Frenchy taps a finger to his nose and points it back at Lauren. "The evolution of all of us, to some extent, but definitely the most current viral evolution of you two. Industry and technology are creeping closer and closer to the viral source."

"It sounds like, regardless of which path Ra follows, the evolution will find a way to happen. Wouldn't he be content with that knowledge?" Dek asks.

"I don't think he has the patience or desire to wait any longer," Frenchy says, again looking out over the harbor.

Before any of them get the chance to comment, the door swings open.

"There you are," says Philippe, leaning out, still holding the doorknob. "Alexander wants to discuss our plan of action."

"Yeah, coming," says Dek, getting up from his seat and cleaning up the plates from their snack.

"We'll be right down, Philippe. Hey, how come I didn't hear you coming just now? I can usually hear people in the hall long before they pop out the door," adds Lauren.

Dek glances at a smiling Frenchy, then back to Philippe. "Yeah, I didn't hear you either."

Philippe replies with a wink. "Some people are just that good."

Lauren shakes her head. "I had a feeling the answer would be something like that."

Philippe gives a nod of his head and exits the terrace, leaving the door open for them.

"How are you feeling about things, Frenchy?" Lauren asks.

"It definitely helped to talk things out," he says, patting her hand. "But I'm not sure that all the talking in the world will avert us from the path we are heading down."

Frenchy remains pensive as Dek and Lauren make their way inside. He pulls out his cell phone and flips through his contacts down to the bottom of the list. He pauses a moment before pressing the call button.

CHAPTER 22

Dek and Lauren walk along the dimly lit passageway to the same ornately carved wooden door to the lower library they entered when they first arrived.

"This may be strange timing, but I was wondering, how do you think our lives will be after all this is over?" Lauren asks with a cautious smile. "Do we start dating, meet each other's families, get nerdy scientist jobs? Where do you see this going?"

Dek stops, turning to face her. "Assuming we survive this whole ordeal, and hopefully Ra's plan to release the virus is stopped, I would love to see where this goes," he replies, gesturing between them.

"I think it would be nice just to be together as a regular couple, doing regular things. I like movies, and I enjoy cooking and reading novels," she responds.

"I like movies too. Sci-fi and action mostly. I love sports and I love to eat. Which goes great with you enjoying cooking," he says with a wink.

"I can endure sports if you will go thrift shopping with me?" she snaps back.

He pulls her in closer. "Sounds like a great life," he says before giving her a quick kiss. "I think we might be late if we don't get moving."

They step upon the threshold, taking time to examine the carvings. Two men are largely prominent, one centered on each door, their closer hands joined at the seam of the two doors, their other hands raised to the sky. A large sun is above their heads, also divided by the seam of the two doors. A stream of relatively faceless people representing various cultures are emerging from the doorframes, also with hands raised to the sun.

"Now that I know some of the story and have met them both, the likenesses are very accurate," says Dek, examining the carving of Victor.

Lauren is standing before the Alexander carving with a slight cringe on her face. "The narcissism portrayed in these carvings is off the charts. They both look like they have a Jesus complex."

As Dek reaches forward for the door handle, the doors swing open.

"Welcome," says Alexander. The large blown-glass sun chandelier seems to glow above his head. It is almost as if the two portrayed in the carvings on the door were replaced with one supreme leader standing under an even more magnificent sun.

Lauren feels a little sick to her stomach as the visual illusion sinks in.

Dek notices her pause and takes her hand. "Thanks, Alexander. The art and imagery of this room is really stunning."

Alexander steps aside, motioning them into the room. "Frenchy had the doors commissioned by a famous local artist in the mid-1950s. They are amazingly well crafted, but they do give one the feeling that we have a god complex," he says wryly.

They walk over to the large table and greet Philippe, Carson, Urvinder, and Thi Thi. Each member of the team has a folder and a laptop in front of them.

"Maria has compiled a folder for you to review, summarizing our plans and how you could potentially help us," Alexander continues, taking his seat at the head of the table. He looks down at the clock on his laptop screen; his face pinches slightly. "It seems that something is keeping Frenchy. Urvinder, would you be so kind as to fill him in upon his return?"

At the same moment, each of the laptops resting on the table fire to life. Each screen contains a map of Colombia and Ecuador. They spend the next hour going over in detail the location of the Helms Chemical dig site and camp, where they expect Ra's forces will attack it from, and how they plan to defend and hopefully shut down the site. Carson is handling most of the transportation concepts, with Thi Thi discussing actual fighting strategies. Philippe will penetrate the camp ahead and be a source of information from within. Dek and Lauren will go in with Carson, mainly supplying backup, if needed, and support for Urvinder, who will stay on the perimeter of the conflict and use her special abilities to neutralize as many people as she can. Cleo and Brutus are already gone, landing in Pasto, Colombia, and meeting with connections that Cleo has from growing up in the area. They hope to have a significant amount of Colombian mercenaries who will approach the camp from the Colombian border and be the primary fighting force if needed. Maria will be in a mobile computer center, coordinating everyone's communications.

After some intense discussions around the specifics of how they believe the fighting could go, Alexander sits back with a confident grin on his face. "I think this sounds good. It's been many years since I've had to plan something like this. It is very invigorating," he says.

Philippe looks over at Urvinder. "So you have been awfully quiet during this whole briefing. What do you think?"

"I am afraid that we are overlooking one significant point in all this. Alexander, what kind of bomb do you think Ra would need to cause significant spray of viral material into the atmosphere, causing the ninth evolution?"

All heads turn back toward Alexander, but they are thinking that they already know the answer to the question.

"It will probably be a nuclear warhead placed deep into the Earth's crust," he says rather matter-of-factly. "If they already have the mines dug to a significant level, he will just need to get the warhead into the mine and set it off."

"If we fail to stop them, everyone near that dig site will die," Urvinder counters in Alexander's same tone.

It is a little traumatic to hear it stated out loud, but they all know that this is a possibility.

"Well, I guess that means we must not fail," says Dek, breaking the tension.

Alexander's computer, almost on cue, draws his attention. "Shit!" is all he says as he adjusts the screen for a better look.

They are all drawn to his reaction, shifting to face him.

Alexander stands. "Frenchy's watch just pinged back to Maria a rapid decline in vitals, ending in a stop to all vitals." He points to Philippe and Carson. "Go find him and find out what's going on."

CHAPTER 23

Philippe and Carson go dashing out, racing for the control room. They burst through the door and find Maria searching multiple computer screens to monitor all of the city's camera feeds.

"I'm hacking into smart cameras to try and spot where they've taken him," she says.

"What do you mean, 'they've taken him'?" says Philippe.

"Frenchy left here and drove to the Griffon; it's a historic Charleston tavern with a secret back room that we have used from time to time for discreet meetings," Maria says, her fingers flying across the keyboard.

Both men lean in toward a map screen scrolling through footage from various street cameras positioned around Charleston. Their advanced brain processing allows them to assess what a regular person would see as a blur.

"How can you even concentrate with all those dollar bills stapled up all over? Money is so dirty. I feel like I can smell every place that each one of those dollar bills has been all at once, and most of them have been in some pretty disgusting places," says Carson, wrinkling his nose.

"There aren't any dollars in the back room," clarifies Philippe.

"You've been there? In the back room?" Carson spits back, looking at his companion.

"I have checked all the surrounding street cameras and it looks like he was meeting Isis. She walked up from the coastal side and entered about five minutes before Frenchy," says Maria, sidestepping Carson's shock.

"Okay, let's go," Carson says, turning for the door.

"Wait! I said he *was* there. I think they have a back exit into a small alley. His watch indicated that he left and got into a car—not his own—and drove to the west side of town. I'm looking through the camera footage to see if I can find him."

"Where was he when the watch said that his vitals had stopped?" asks Philippe, also scanning the monitors.

"He was here." She slides over to a different computer and brings up a map of Charleston with a small dot blinking on what looks like a rural, unpopulated stretch of road. "There aren't any street cameras in that area."

"So his watch stopped moving for about one minute and then his vitals dropped?" Philippe asks, eyeing the watch readouts on the side of the map screen.

"Yes," says Maria, furiously typing on a laptop.

"That really doesn't sound good," adds Carson.

Dek and Lauren rush over just behind the other two, concerned but trying to stay out of the way. "Any news?" Lauren asks.

"Nothing fucking good," replies Carson, looking stressed.

"There!" says Maria, pointing to the screen on her laptop. "I was able to hack into the private cameras of the person who owns the land on the other side of the road."

"That must be where the car stopped." Philippe points to a gravel spot across the road from the camera. "Is this now? Can we go back to when it was there?" he asks Maria.

"I'm trying to pull that up now," she replies. "Live feed and feed history are stored at different sites in the system."

The feed starts to zoom backward. They see the car pull away and back up to when it arrived.

"Oh shit! I hope I didn't see what I thought I just saw," says Carson, pulling his hand across his face.

The whole group is staring as the feed starts up just after the car arrives. The car sits on the gravel, idling. The camera angle is toward the back window of the car. They can kind of make out that the driver is turning, maybe talking to someone in the back seat. The driver turns back to the front, then angrily gets out and walks to the back driver's side door. Isis is clearly the driver, her curly dark hair flowing about her face. She yanks open the back door of the car. They watch in horror as she raises a pistol and shoots three shots into the back seat. The rear passenger side window is blown out by one of the bullets. A small head is barely visible in the back window just before the shots are fired.

They all just stare in silence as Isis returns to the driver's seat, backs out, and pulls away down the street. Maria pauses the feed just after the car pulls out of frame.

There are tears streaming down Lauren's face, her eyes wide in shock. "Oh my god. I've never seen anything like that before in real life," she says quietly.

Dek turns to her and wraps her in his arms. His own eyes tear up as he thinks, *We were just talking a few hours ago.*

"Can you go back to just before the shots were fired and zoom in on the back window? I just want to see if we can get a facial confirmation," says Philippe.

Alexander, Thi Thi, and Urvinder walk up outside the computer room.

"I'm not sure that you want to see this," Dek says quietly.

"I just had a conversation with Ra," Alexander says somberly. "He claimed that Frenchy contacted him, offering to corrupt us from the inside in exchange for Ra not forcing the release of the virus."

In silence, they stare and shake their heads.

"Ra said he had Isis execute Frenchy on our behalf for his treason," Alexander continues, his tone barely disguising his brimming anger. "He will return the body to us after a full debriefing once he's back in the country next week, so we can properly make arrangements for the funeral."

"He's so full of shit!" yells Carson. "We would be taking care of funeral arrangements while his team in Ecuador is triggering the ninth evolution."

Maria turns from her screen; it is frozen on the zoom in of the car's back window, just before the shots are fired. It clearly shows a panicked Frenchy glancing out the back window, desperately looking for help or a way out.

Philippe turns away from the screen after verifying his suspicion. "Goddamnit, French," he says to himself.

Alexander clears his throat. "I think our path is clear. We must not be deterred. I believe that Frenchy did what he did to try and end this conflict or at least buy us some time. I can't believe that he could have anticipated Ra's actions."

"You're right, we can't let his sacrifice be in vain," adds Dek.

"Frenchy's welcoming smile and demeanor are the most comforting things I've experienced," says Lauren. *With so much pressure, and the fate of the world seemingly hanging in the balance. A little "my friends," delivered with a smile, even if it wasn't completely genuine, was a comfort*, thinks Lauren.

"Everyone take some time to process all this. We'll meet tomorrow and finalize our plans," says Alexander, and he and Thi Thi leave.

Urvinder pauses a moment longer, looking at the video as Philippe runs it back and forth, tightly examining each frame.

Dek and Lauren walk quietly back to their room. Once inside, Dek flops down on the bed with his hands behind his head, and Lauren slumps down in an oversize chair just next to him.

"Do you think that our discussion with Frenchy caused him to go to Ra?" Dek asks, staring up at the coffered ceiling.

After a brief silence, Lauren says, "Maybe, but I think he would have done it anyway. I think in some ways he was still trying to decide if he was on the right team."

Dek looks over to her. "You think he was with Ra?"

She shakes her head. "No, I think he is with all of them, both sides. I think he believes more in what Alexander is standing for but he has a greater affinity for Ra."

"I guess I could see that. Ra does have a point."

Lauren shifts forward in her seat. "Are you ready to risk your life for this?"

Decklan keeps his eyes focused on the ceiling. "I just can't stand by and have a virus released on this world that could kill half of the population. If I can do something, anything, then I have to try."

She gets up and crawls into bed, snuggling her head into his chest.

"I'm sorry that happened," he says, kissing her head and wrapping his arm around her. "I know you liked him. Did you want to get some sleep so that we are ready in the morning?"

"No, I really want to forget all this for a few hours," she replies and inches her face up to kiss him.

CHAPTER 24

It's been twenty-four hours since they landed in Colombia. Brutus and Cleo are bouncing along a pothole-riddled road near the southern border with Ecuador. Cleo's "brother" is in the passenger seat, guiding them to a small encampment just north of the border.

Cleo refers to Miguel as her brother, but he is actually her grandson. She gave birth to Miguel's mother when she was in her teens and had her interaction with the virus shortly after. Cleo's ability to keep her cells looking young make her look more like she's thirty-five than her biological age of seventy-eight, so it makes sense for society to view her as his sister.

Their truck rounds a corner and the jungle overgrowth opens into a small village with lots of run-down huts and homes. Chickens and goats roam freely about the streets. After about a mile they come up to a large wooden fence. Two guards with machine guns are sitting at a beat-up table playing cards. They stop the game and pick up their guns as the truck pulls up. Miguel speaks to them briefly and hands them some money. One of the guards makes a call on his cell phone. After a few seconds, the guards open the gate and allow the truck to pass.

Beyond the gate is a well-manicured estate. There is a large Spanish-style home at the top of a curving driveway. Midway up the paved drive, Cleo directs the truck toward a six-doored structure with a housing unit over the top of it. There are at least ten men in the garage: some working on cars or trucks, others just hanging out. "Ramon can be a little particular about parking in front of his doorway," she explains.

They get out and approach the front door of the main house. "You did leave all your weapons in the car, didn't you?" Miguel asks before knocking.

"For the most part," confirms Cleo with a smile.

"If I have to, I can fight my way out," says Brutus, giving him a wink.

"They may not even let you in with your size," Miguel jokes.

The door is eventually yanked open by a man wearing tan pants and a billowing white shirt. His shirt is hanging open, revealing an elaborate tattoo of a Spanish woman, which momentarily distracts them from the sawed-off shotgun he is casually holding.

"Hey, Ramon, you remember my sister Cleo?" Miguel asks nervously. "And this is her man, Brutus."

Ramon's cagey stare flits over the group. He offers them a small jerk of his chin in greeting and leans his shoulder on the doorframe, blocking their entrance and view of the interior of his home. "Miguel tells me you have a business proposition for me?" he says.

Cleo steps forward. "We have intel that high explosives, which will have a direct impact on your operation here, will be used at a nearby dig site. We would like your help to put this project out of commission."

"So you are here to warn me of impending danger?" His eyes narrow. "You have come all this way out of concern for me and the people in this town?" he asks.

The calmness of his heartbeat tells Cleo that he is not looking to hurt them but simply wants honesty. Her lips quirk up in a slight you've-caught-me smile, and she nods. "We have known each other for many years, Ramon, so I will be as honest with you as I can be, mi amigo. May we come inside?"

Repeatedly tapping his thumb on the gun, Ramon turns his distrustful gaze to Brutus's formidable form, weighing the potential threat. Finally, he straightens to his full height and, using the barrel of the gun, waves them inside.

**

"And this technetium," Cleo says, sitting on the edge of a large leather couch, "has a radiation signature that is holding a deadly virus dormant .... We have reliable intel that another group wants to release this virus."

Brutus uncrosses his long legs and leans forward. "They want to set a large bomb in the dig site and cause the release of the virus worldwide, which could cause the deaths of millions or even billions of people."

Ramon purses his brow and attempts to wave them off. "This sounds like something for governments to handle," he says, "not a group of mercenaries."

"Well," Cleo says, placing her coffee mug on the table in front of them, "we don't want to cause a worldwide panic. And getting governments involved could do just that."

Ramon concedes the truth of that statement with a dip of his chin. "*Eso es verdad.*"

"We think the group attacking the site will be a small force, twenty or thirty people," Brutus says. "The group defending the site will probably be about forty to fifty. With your help, we believe this could be done with minimal casualties and kept relatively quiet."

Ramon's gaze flickers over their faces. "My first thought was what's in it for me. But this virus you speak of ... millions or billions of deaths ..."

"Sí" is all Cleo says.

Ramon stands. "If we are going to do this together in a very tight time window, I hope you have a plan," he says, walking toward a bar at the back of the house. He peers out his back window and pours four shots of tequila. "Come, mis amigos, let's drink to our upcoming success."

Cleo's phone starts to buzz as soon as they put down their empty shot glasses. She looks down at the screen. "Ramon, this is the rest of our team. Are you okay with me taking this call?" she asks.

Ramon nods and motions the men to follow him. "Brutus, Miguel, let me show you the grounds."

"Hello," she answers. "Yes, Alexander, Ramon is willing to help. I will need a copy of the plans that you have drawn up, the amount of men needed, and the timeline," she fires off so quickly that he doesn't have a chance to speak.

"That's great news, Cleo," Alexander says, the grimness in his tone unmistakable.

"What's wrong?" she asks immediately, bracing for bad news with one hand on the bar.

"Frenchy's dead," he says softly. "Isis killed him."

Cleo feels the air get knocked out of her. "No ...." she says, clutching her stomach, then reaching for a place to sit down.

Brutus glances back at her from the patio and does a double take. He starts walking back toward her.

"I'm so sorry to have to tell you over the phone," Alexander says, pausing to draw a breath. "We must keep moving forward, though. I truly believe that is what Frenchy would want." He clears his throat and shifts the phone to his other ear. "Ra's dissembling makes us believe he will attack within a week. I am forwarding the plans to you and sending the rest of the team tomorrow."

"Yes, sir" is all Cleo can muster before ending the call.

Brutus walks through the back door. "Babe, are you okay?" he asks, kneeling at her side.

"Isis murdered Frenchy," she says flatly and falls forward into his embrace.

CHAPTER 25

The sun is creeping up into the sky, breaking the jungle tree line at the Helms Chemical mining camp in Ecuador. A few of the men are making their way to the mess tent to the left of the command hut; others are getting the equipment ready for the day. The lights have been on in the command hut for some time now. Helms is typing away on his laptop.

"Coffee, Mr. Helms?" asks an attendant, poking his head through the open, screened doorway.

"Ah, yeah, sure," replies Helms without looking up. "Dammit, I miss being on the East Coast," he says to himself. "I had all of my morning computer routine set up to revolve around when East Coasters were getting on. I'm all thrown off here."

Feldman intercepts the mug from the attendant as he enters the command hut.

"I have your coffee, sir," he says, setting the cup down and taking the seat on the other side of the desk. He waits quietly for Helms to acknowledge him.

Helms takes a sip and grimaces. "Coffee's trash here."

"At least it's hot," Feldman says with a shrug.

"Everything in this jungle is hot … and humid. I can't wait to be done with this."

"About that, sir," starts Feldman, "we can start blasting this afternoon. We are still too high in the crust layer to get at the metal, but the blasting that we do today will open the path to the layers below. Once we clear away the rubble, our crews can easily dig down to the metal. If we get underway as expected, the rubble can be removed in two days."

"So we should have the metal being mined in five days?" Helms clarifies.

"Yes, or sooner, but I know that you want special care taken not to damage the run of ore."

"The ore must be mined out. We can't risk losing our product due to haste," says Helms. He gulps down some more coffee before sliding the mug away in disgust. "So did you hear any more from that investor who was snooping around?" he asks casually.

"Oh, Miss Olivia? Yes, we had a brief follow-up lunch," Feldman says, squirming uneasily in his seat. "I do think she has the capital to invest, but I don't think that there is a lot of benefit to us in a joint endeavor."

"What sort of things did she ask you about our operations?" Helms asks.

"I think she got the gist of it from the meeting that we all had together," Feldman answers. Trying not to smile, he adds, "Most of the time she was asking about me, getting to know me."

Helms just stares at him.

"I mean, I guess she asked a few questions about our operations," Feldman stammers. "But she did ask about my interests and hobbies outside of work ...." Seeing Helms's growing disappointment, Feldman decides to just shut up.

"I think that she was entirely too smart to be worried about your hobbies," Helms bluntly tells him. "She spoke with the cunning of a trained lawyer. If I had to guess, in between blabbering about your stamp collections, she snuck in some pretty leading questions about our operation. I'm not sure what her real reason for being here is, but we need to get moving as fast as we can."

"Of course, sir," Feldman replies, feeling like a fool.

Helms resumes typing on his computer, only to pause after a few keystrokes. *The disappearance of Thomas and Summers, this Olivia suddenly showing up with an investment opportunity, something is not adding up.* His gut never led him wrong when it came to his business dealings. *I would be smart to trust it now.*

"Feldman!" Helms calls as Feldman heads for the door.

"Yes, sir."

"I had a small attachment of men from the Heretic Group sent to Quito in case we need some heavy hitters," he says. "Please contact them and have them repositioned here. There are too many questions in the air to be ignored."

CHAPTER 26

Dek and Lauren are packing two large, black duffel bags with the things they'll need in Ecuador.

"At least we aren't getting kidnapped this time," Dek jokes, putting some shirts in his bag.

"Yeah, we actually get to calmly pack for ourselves for a change," Lauren yells back, then walks out of the bathroom with some of her toiletries. She stops and looks at him. "What's up?" she asks, sensing something is off from the way he's looking at her.

He takes the items from her and sets them in her bag, urging her to sit on the bed. "Before we head out into whatever craziness Ecuador has in store for us, I wanted to tell you ... well, that having you here, to go through all of this with, has really meant the world to me." He pauses, takes her hands, and looks into her eyes. "I know it hasn't been very long, but I feel like I've grown so close to you, and I need you to know ... well ... that I love you."

Lauren blows out a breath. "I thought there was more bad news coming," she says, relief clear on her face. She wraps her arms around his neck and kisses him passionately. Pulling back with her arms still in place and a huge smile on her face, she says, "I love you too."

A quick knock at the door interrupts them. "Are you guys ready to go?" Carson yells.

"Just give us a few more minutes," Lauren yells back before diving back into another long kiss with Dek.

* * *

Philippe and Urvinder are whispering when Dek and Lauren see them in the hallway. Philippe waves, then heads down the stairs while Urvinder waits for them.

"Can I help you with any of your things?" Dek asks as they approach her.

She smiles. "No, thank you. Carson already grabbed my bag from my room."

"Urvinder, I wondered if I could ask you a rather delicate question?" Lauren says nervously, picking at a cuticle as they descend the stairs together.

"Yes, my dear, what is it?"

"When we went to the meeting the other day in the lower library, I was looking at the big carved door. It kind of looks like Alexander and Victor are holding hands. Is there, er, a conflict of interest here that could impact what we are about to undertake?"

Urvinder shakes her head. "Ha, there are many conflicts of interest here, my child. That is not one of them."

"So Ra and Alexander never had a romantic relationship?" Lauren prods as they reach the landing.

"Not that I know of. Having known Victor for so many years, I do believe his romantic interest is slanted more toward men than women, but they appeared to just be friends. The library picture is supposed to show them joined in unity, leading the human race into the next phase of evolution under the sun. In fact, it is more accurate to say that the conflict between them is over a woman."

"What do you mean?" asks Dek.

"Let's go sit in there so this old lady can rest her bones, then I'll tell you the story," Urvinder says, directing them to the kitchen.

"So, back in the sixties, a young and very driven lawyer—newly licensed, as a matter-of-fact—caught Alexander's eye. Even with a huge, almost one-hundred-year age gap between them, they began a passionate love affair. In a nutshell, her hold over Alexander was so complete that it alone almost drove Ra and Alexander apart," Urvinder says gruffly. She wiggles to situate herself more comfortably in the chair. "Where was I? Right ... well, in the years that followed, she quit her job as a lawyer and became a large part of the Children of the Sun, even though she herself was not evolved. This was also around the time that Victor was finishing his evolutionary timeline. He had for many years been experimenting on using blood transfusions from evolved humans to change over those who did not have contact with the virus, achieving mixed results. The worst of those being that over half of the people he experimented on died. Alexander was disgusted by these experiments and forced Victor to stop—"

"Wait, you mean Victor would do infusions on people without telling them the risks they were taking?" Dek is appalled.

Urvinder's head wavers side to side. "Usually he would coerce them into doing the experiment by showing them all that they could become if they had the right genome and by downplaying the risks. This was generally effective in that, if someone tried and was noncompatible, they were dead and couldn't dissuade others from trying. Anyway, Victor agreed to stop the experiments, for the most part. But that damn woman ..." Urvinder nearly growls. "She kept asking Alexander to allow Victor to experiment on her. Her drive and desire to be more was unquenchable, but Alexander forbade it. The risk of losing her was too great for him.

"Soon, though, a larger rift formed between the men, mainly due to Victor's obsession with causing the ninth. While Alexander was working to keep the team together, his love began reading everything she could get her hands on in the library. She became very close with Frenchy and, through him, gained full access to Victor's work and his timeline. One night when a newly evolved young man was brought to us with injuries, she transfused herself with his evolved blood.

"The next morning when the sun came up, she ventured out into the gardens and collapsed on the cobblestones. Alexander found her, the shock nearly stopping his own heart. She was fine—she had evolved—but the fact that she was so careless with her life almost drove Alexander to the brink. He blamed Frenchy at first, but Victor convinced him that it was his conversations with her and her belief in his timeline that pushed her to the decision. That was the final straw. Alexander kicked Victor out of the group and, much to Alexander's dismay, others chose to leave with Victor—including the love of Alexander's life."

"Alexander's love ... it's Osiris, isn't it?" asks Dek.

Urvinder looks at him in surprise. "Yes, actually." She sighs. "I sometimes feel that she runs the Evos as much as Victor does."

"When I was being held by the Evos, Osiris wanted to discuss whether people of different backgrounds and situations would choose to evolve if they knew the odds of the evolutionary virus. I never would have guessed that she was one of those people." He looks at Lauren. "Imagine ... she chose to risk death to be evolved. Bit hard to wrap your head around that, yeah?"

Lauren nods. "I guess I could understand if she were ill or something, but to be so driven to risk it all. That's crazy."

Urvinder gets to her feet. "Interesting tidbit ... it wouldn't surprise me to learn those two are still in love today, separated only by their pride and stubbornness."

"Hmm, do you think we could be in danger if Alexander is not willing to do what is necessary to stop Osiris?" Dek asks.

"Only time will tell." Urvinder begins to head out of the kitchen just as Carson peeks his head in.

"Urvinder, it's time to go; your car is here," he tells her.

Dek and Lauren turn abruptly toward Urvinder. "Are you not going with us to Ecuador?" Lauren asks at the exact moment Dek says, "You're not coming with us?"

Urvinder chuckles. "No, I am nearly two hundred years old. The time for me to fight real fights is almost over. I'm not sure that I could even make it through the jungle to the dig site, to be completely honest." She walks back and gives them both a hug. "Your hearts are true, you will fight bravely, and what will be will be."

CHAPTER 27

A line of three trucks pulls up to an abandoned warehouse on the east side of Tulcan, a city north of Quito. The Hispanic drivers of the first two trucks get out and walk toward a bank of semi-sized garage doors. Two of the garage doors start to inch open as the men approach. Anubis is standing just inside the first door, holding the opener.

"We have fifteen men who were able to take the blood transfusion and evolve," says the first man.

"Drive over to that large spot of open land," Anubis says, pointing to the far side of the garage. "Deposit the bodies in the trenches and have the evolved men bury them. When it's done, come inside and get some food. We have some planning to do."

The second man nods, and the two men return to the trucks, waving for the third truck to follow.

"Fraternizing with the cannon fodder?" quips Isis as she walks up behind Anubis.

"Look, mate, it feels to me like we're all cannon fodder," he replies, looking up toward Osiris talking on her phone just outside the lofted office space. "Well, almost all of us."

"How much do you want to bet that she won't even show up to take down the camp?" Isis whispers.

"I'm fine with that, she's more brain than brawn. A complete liability in a scrum. All I care about is getting out of there before the bomb goes off, and that's what I need from her," Anubis says flatly. "I ain't down for suicide missions."

"I guess that's why we have those jokers in the trucks," she says, glancing to the back of the building.

It takes about a half hour for the trucks to pull back around. There is a large table loaded with food at the back of the warehouse. The men rush straight toward it as soon as they enter the doors. Anubis looks over the group of men as they devour their food. He then climbs the staircase to the office where Isis and Osiris are sitting around a large desk. "Bloody hell, those boys' cells are buzzing like a swarm of bees," he says as he closes the door. "I don't think they have much, if any, military training, but they'll cause a good distraction."

Osiris is distracted herself, by an image she's studying on her laptop. She motions him to sit and slowly tears her gaze from the monitor to focus on Anubis and Isis. "We should probably go over the plans again." She points to the men downstairs. "So they will drive the three trucks into the camp, but most of them will be in the first two trucks. We're going to let them flood out throughout the camp. Once the excitement begins, if the way is clear, you two will continue to drive the third truck right through the camp, heading for the dig site. You will have a four-wheeler parked in the back of the truck, loaded with the bomb. Drive the four-wheeler straight down to the mouth of the dig site." Osiris turns the laptop around so they can view the satellite image. "Two days ago these miners fired off some smaller explosives; they have been clearing the debris since. Get to the site, unload the explosive, and I'll pick you up here"—she taps the extraction point—"in the clearing on the far side of the dig site, about one hundred feet into the jungle."

"Then BOOM." Anubis imitates an explosion. "And the world will never be the same."

"This is what we have been training for," Osiris says. "Stick to the plan and we've got it in the bag."

Isis drags the laptop closer to examine the image. "Is this the latest?"

Osiris nods and reaches out to stack the various papers scattered on the desk.

"It looks like they've beefed up security a bit."

"I think this latest step forward in their mining process has them closer to their goal, and they want to protect it," Osiris replies.

Anubis peers over Isis's shoulder to look at the image she's examining. "Can you play the footage?" he asks.

"Sure." She taps one of the laptop keys, causing the still image to come to life.

After a few minutes of watching, the guards walk around.

"Love, these aren't the same guards they've had patrolling," Anubis says. "It's not all of them, but at least three that I can see here are military trained." He points to one of the spots moving on the screen. "I've been studying their movements for the last few weeks and I can usually see regular missteps in their patrol lines. This bloke here hasn't missed a step."

"We did see the arrival of five new men the day after they started blasting," Osiris says. "I had assumed they were heavy-machine operators brought in to clear the debris field."

"No, love, these are trained mercs. I don't know if it changes a lot of what we are planning, but we do need to take it into account." Anubis scratches the scruff on his neck. "You said five of them arrived? They will put at least two at the control hut and the other three are probably the ones I can pick out on the sat, in key patrol locations. If it seems that taking the control hut is our main goal, that will probably draw the lot of them. I suggest we send the first truck directly to the control hut and the other toward the side of the camp farthest from the dig site. If we can keep all of the action there, we'll have a better shot at our true goal."

"Good observation," says Osiris. "I like this plan! They'll think our objective is to take control of the camp and mine the metal for ourselves. That should divert most of their defenses away from our main target."

Anubis slides the laptop over to her and sits back.

"Our best chance of successfully causing the ninth is for the bomb to go off as close to noon as possible," Osiris reminds them. "A high sun location will expose the most viral particles to the stimulus they need for activation."

"Affirmative," Isis says with a quick bob of her head. "Any word from Ra? Did our little distraction keep the Children at home?"

"As far as I know, some of them. The rest of them are very motivated by that stunt," replies Osiris.

"I think that's got to be our biggest concern. Hopefully we're moving faster than they were able to, and we can be in and out before they even get here. I'd rather not fight the highly trained and evolved if we can avoid it."

"If the Children get involved, their goal will be twofold: first stopping us, and then stopping Helms Chemical from doing any more digging," adds Anubis. "If we can get them fighting the Helms Chemical guys instead of us, that would be a huge win."

Osiris grins. "Ra may have a trick or two up his sleeve when it comes to his old group," she says cryptically.

"Right then," Anubis says with a rap of his knuckles on the table. "Isis and I will go down, prepare the vehicles, and inform the men of our plans. Try to get a little shut-eye, mate."

Anubis and Isis stop at the bottom of the stairs, moving out of sight and earshot. "So you can see where this is going. It's you and me out in the fight," Anubis whispers. "That sheila isn't even puttin' boots on the ground for this one. She is so obsessed with causing this to happen—maybe just to justify her own decisions—if she sees any signs of failure, she might set the bomb off before we can get out."

"Aye, and the stakes are too high for Ra to stop," Isis says. "If we are close but can't get to the pickup zone, she'll not hesitate to set off the bomb. Even if it's still in our hands."

"There are two ways to set off the bomb, timer and remote detonation. I'm of the thinking that if we deactivate her remote device, then the only way it goes boom is if we set it off," says Anubis.

"Hmm." Isis scratches her nose, then points at him. "What if we rig our own remote detonation device? That way she has to get us out before we set it off."

Anubis nods rapidly. "I like it. She will have a detonator that is set to nothing, and we will have the real one. We'll tell her once we are in the camp so she knows she has to pick us up."

"Now all we have to do is fight through a small army of men and potentially our old team, set the bomb in the dig site, and get to the extraction area. Piece of cake," she says with a shrug.

Anubis throws his arm around her shoulder. "We've been in a lot of tough scraps before and have come out on top every time!"

CHAPTER 28

At six p.m. two large trucks pull into Ramon's compound. Cleo and Brutus come out to greet them while Ramon stands up on his porch area, cradling his shotgun and shifting his gaze back and forth warily.

Carson jumps down from the driver's side of the first truck and grabs Brutus's big mitt, pulling him in for a half hug. "You ready for this, bro?" he asks.

"Just waiting for you jokers, mate," Brutus replies.

Philippe, Dek, Lauren, and Thi Thi exit the second truck. Maria, who was riding with Carson, waves from the passenger seat, testing the satellite links from her laptop.

Cleo looks around the group as Brutus introduces them to Ramon and Miguel. "I'm pleasantly surprised to see you, Thi Thi," she says. "I thought you'd be staying with Alexander. But where is Urvinder?"

"She didn't think she could navigate the jungle, felt like she'd be more of a hindrance than an asset," says Thi Thi with a frown.

Cleo shakes her head. "She could never be. Okay, I may have to alter our plans without her particular talents."

"I think Frenchy's death ..." begins Philippe. "Well, Urvinder was very quiet about it. I think it hit her hard ...."

Silence fills the air. The group's sadness is palpable as Ramon motions them into the house.

"Is Maria okay?" Brutus asks Carson as they walk in.

"She is in full panic mode," he says, looking back at her still typing furiously in the truck. "She is trying to establish her satellite link. If she can't get that to work, I'm not sure any of her tech will function."

"Sounds like me when my home Wi-Fi goes out. Unplug and wait for a minute, then reboot the modem. Really fucking frustrating," says Brutus.

Throwing an arm around the bigger man, Carson says, "Yeah, better just to let her be."

Ramon ushers them into a room with a large table laden with food. They all hungrily fix themselves a plate and sit. Philippe, sitting at the very end of the table near Cleo and Brutus, says, "I've got us about fifty miles from the dig site. We need to eat, get a bit of rest, and then head out in the early morning. Once we gauge the camp's defenses, we'll need to decide if we should take the camp over and defend it, or let the camp defend itself and only come in if they are overwhelmed."

"I already did some recon of the dig camp," Cleo says. "They are armed, and it appears that they have added more experienced forces in just the last week. Osiris's first logical move would be on-site recon, maybe she tipped her hand during her attempts to get into the camp."

"Do we know who's in charge?" Philippe asks.

"I think it's the head of the company, a Mr. Helms," says Brutus.

Dek and Lauren look at each other. Dek raises his finger in the air. "That guy—Helms—was our colleague's stepfather," Dek says. "My understanding is that he's a bit of an asshole."

"He was also the man who hired Lauren to test the dig-site samples that led to your evolution, is he not?" Philippe asks before taking another bite of his empanada.

"Yes, but we believe that what he is truly after is the metal's radiation for weapons guidance systems," Lauren says, easing into the conversation. "If he feels that there is a threat, it would be the threat of another company or government trying to take over his site to take the metal for themselves."

Philippe finishes chewing, with his gaze focused on Dek and Lauren. "He had a man chasing you from Wisconsin to North Carolina. Did you have a sample of the metal or specifics about the metal or the origin of the samples? What was he after?"

"I sent all of the radiated samples back to Helms the day of the accident that changed us," Lauren says, shaking her head. "I was literally getting the supplies to do a final cleanup of the area when the accident occurred, so I'm not one hundred percent sure why that man was trying to kill us."

Dek shrugs. "Yeah, I don't think Helms knew anything about the fact that we had evolved. That was the main reason we were able to defeat his guy, Vince, in the end."

"Do you think he was just trying to tie up loose ends?" asks Cleo.

"Well, when we were at Dr. Strong's lab in Chicago, he was looking for that filter we recovered from the hood," Dek points out.

"Did the filter contain any fragments of radiated metal?" asks Philippe.

"No, I did a really thorough cleaning of any radiated contaminate," Lauren says. "It could possibly have had viral particles on it, though …. I wasn't looking for that during my initial cleanup."

"After the bomb at Dr. Strong's lab didn't take you out, I'll bet he was just trying to cover his tracks," says Philippe, recalling his surveillance of them while determining if they had evolved.

"You're right. We could identify him at that point," confirms Lauren.

"I'm just trying to determine if his pursuit of you could be related to your evolution or just your knowledge of what he was doing," Philippe says. "I guess it doesn't matter in the end. What is more pertinent is if he can mount an effective defense of the camp. We definitely want to shut down the mine and the dig overall, but if the Evos manage to blow up the dig site, that would be endgame—"

"And endgame for all of us sitting in the blast radius," interjects Brutus.

Philippe curses under his breath, then nods. "Okay, I've changed my mind about our options. The plan is we wait for the Evos to attack. I think it would be too difficult to take the camp and hold it. If they attack before we are settled, they would have us."

"The camp *is* already set to defend itself," Thi Thi says in agreement. "We just have to hope the defenses stand long enough for us to reinforce their efforts."

Philippe peers at each of his colleagues around the table. "I am expecting a full-out assault on the dig site. It is the real goal, not the camp." He points to Cleo, Brutus, and Thi Thi. "You three will set up near the dig site. You must not let Anubis or Isis near the site. Carson, you stay with Maria and be her backup. Lauren, Dek, and I will try and contain the Evos in the main part of the camp—"

"Don't forget, I have ten men willing to assist you," Ramon interrupts from the far end of the table. "They are brave men, but you should all know that they are only adequately trained."

"The help is greatly appreciated. Let's be prepared to make changes on-site if the conditions change." Philippe adds.

Heads around the table bob in acknowledgment just as a figure appears in the doorway. All eyes land on Maria.

She gives them an awkward half wave. "Hiya," she says and quickly scans the food options. Her hand hovers over several items before she makes a selection and grabs the closest seat.

"Right, so Ramon's men will come with Lauren, Dek, and me," Philippe continues. "If we can keep the Evos from getting to the actual dig site, it's a win."

"What would happen if the bomb is set off before they get to the dig site?" Miguel asks.

"To be honest, that might be a solution to all our problems," Carson says. "It would destroy and effectively shut down the camp. The dig site would most likely collapse in on itself, stopping any progress they have thus far made."

Philippe looks thoughtfully at him. "The political ramifications of the disaster would cause the Ecuadorean government to have second thoughts about allowing this kind of mining, possibly halting any future people trying to mine for the metal in the region—"

"It would also be the death of all of us, the people at the camp, and the Evos," says Cleo.

"Jesús, María, y José," Ramon murmurs. "I will be evacuating my compound, just in case."

"I think I like the plan where we stop the Evos and halt the Helms Chemical mining project, harm minimal people, and all get back alive," Dek says with a smile.

"Hear! Hear!" erupts around the table.

Once they settle down again, Thi Thi turns to Ramon. "You mentioned the camp is using laborers from here ... can we use their transportation routes to get closer?"

"Yes, there is a group of workers who come from some of the nearby villages to work at the site," he says. "They arrive in the morning and leave for home in the evening. I'm sure you could get a man into the site by sneaking in with that group."

"Not a bad idea," says Philippe. "I could certainly modify my look enough to pull it off. Having someone already on the grounds is a big advantage."

"Then me, Dek, and Ramon's men will reinforce you if the Evos attack," confirms Lauren.

Philippe inclines his head toward her. "Yes, you can all stay with Carson and Maria in her mobile computer center until needed." He looks at Ramon. "Maria's truck will be positioned about fifty feet into the jungle from the camp. That's where she'll be organizing our defenses and keeping our movements coordinated."

Ramon absorbs the information with a nod.

"I think this sounds good, but we must be open to improvisation," Brutus says. "When the bullets start to fly, even the best plans can get thrown out the window."

Philippe stands. "One last toast to our success, then we all need to get what rest we can."

They all stand up and clink glasses, with nervous smiles and a hail of good lucks.

Slowly, the group begins to disperse. Ramon points Dek and Lauren to a couch on the screened porch looking out over the back patio. They are surprised to see Brutus already there, sitting in a rocking chair, quietly rocking. He is looking around, tapping his thick fingers on the armrest.

"Sorry, mates. I am just waiting for Cleo to finish up with her grandson."

They follow his line of sight across the patio to two figures on the lawn praying, their hands closed together in front of them with heads bowed.

"I guess it seems kind of funny, but after all this evolution and science talk, I haven't thought much about the faith side of all this," says Dek.

"Miguel has yet to be exposed to the virus," Brutus says soberly. "The odds that he could survive the ninth are not great. Cleo has always had a very strong belief in God and Jesus. She believes that only through faith will we as a people be able to get through something like the ninth evolution."

They watch Cleo and Miguel stand and hug before he leaves. She walks across the patio and enters through the sliding screen door. "Why is everyone so quiet?" she asks.

"We were each caught in a little introspective thought," says Lauren.

"Don't worry, my friends," Cleo says with a wink. "I made sure to put in a word for you too. He will be with us tomorrow," she assures them.

CHAPTER 29

After a short rest, the Children of the Sun are up at three in the morning and moving into place. Maria's truck is set up about fifty feet off the camp's main path—the one used by the workers Philippe plans to blend in with to infiltrate said camp. Dek, Lauren, and Ramon's men wait at the truck with Maria and Carson, planning to move in at the first sign of trouble. Maria is using her satellite connection to access real-time footage to try and track movement in the area as Brutus, Cleo, and Thi Thi get positioned closer to the actual dig site, finding a spot five feet into the jungle foliage. They will be the last line of defense if the Evos get all the way through the camp to the dig site.

At around six a.m., the sun starts to rise and beams of light start peeking through the jungle canopy.

"I have a new satellite coming into range," Maria says, typing away on her keyboard. A wide shot of the Ecuadorean region of South America pops up on her screen. She zooms in on some roads to the camp that she has highlighted as the main possible routes for the Evos to follow.

"There!" says Carson, looking over Maria's shoulder and pointing to a spot on the display. "Movement ... Wait, they just went under that lot of trees."

"Okay, I got it," says Maria, zooming in a little more. The small convoy of three trucks emerges from the tree branches covering the road heading toward the camp. "I think they are about two hours out. They should be here just as the sun fully starts to cover the camp with light."

"Inform Philippe through his earpiece," Carson tells her.

"Is their timing important with the positioning of the sun?" asks Lauren.

"Yes, if Ra sticks to his normal MO, they will have used evolved blood to create newly evolved soldiers to help them," Carson says. "These soldiers will definitely be stronger in direct sunlight. Additionally, if they are able to set off the explosive, the sun will increase the virus's virulence."

"Could an explosion in one location *really* cause the virus to spread across the globe?" Lauren asks. "I'm picturing the blast radius of a sneeze or cough in a crowded restaurant .... It's still limited to a two- or three-table area."

Carson shrugs. "To be honest, Ra and Frenchy were the real experts when it comes to the virus, but they believed that it could happen."

"The evolutionary virus is different than viruses like the flu or Ebola. You really can't think of the transmission as being the same. Once released into the upper atmosphere, it should proliferate and cover the globe in hours. In a few days it should all be over except for the cleanup," Maria states rather coldly.

* * *

"Looks like we are in for good weather," Feldman says as he walks into the command hut with his computer bag slung over his shoulder. "The site excavation should go smoothly," he adds as he sets down two cups of fresh coffee on the table.

Helms stops typing to grab a coffee. "It's going to be sunny today?" he asks, taking a sip. "Alert the guards to be extra attentive. The sun can cause them to get lethargic as the day drones on." He stands and walks out to the deck, leaning on the front railing and looking out over the camp. The guards are directing the workers to their tasks as the camp starts to buzz with activity. Multiple trucks are firing to life, disturbing the calm of the jungle. After a few moments of observation, Helms returns to his seat.

Feldman logs on and checks his email. "Yes, I'll be talking to the security head in thirty. I did receive another inquiry from Olivia Osiris. She is requesting another meeting, trying to sweeten the deal and get in on our dig site location."

"When did she request the meeting?" Helms asks.

"Well, she was pushing to meet with us today, around noon," Feldman says, checking his watch.

"That's rather aggressive," says Helms, again glancing out the window. He can hear the trucks pulling out and leaving for the dig site. "I do like that kind of confidence, but we have too much going on here."

"Of course, sir, you're right. I'll email her that we can set up a meeting for another day."

"Or not at all. The success we are on the brink of will change our fortunes forever, Feldman. Let's not worry too much about sharing it with anyone just yet. If this goes as planned, we'll have a marketing team sharing our products with potential buyers within a year," Helms says with an anticipatory smile.

"I will email her back that we are not interested," Feldman says, rather disappointed in not seeing Olivia again. Fifteen minutes later, he gets up to leave. "I am off to my meeting."

"Oh, Feldman," Helms calls out, "could you have the guards question all of the workers who came in this morning? I don't want to take any chances ...."

"Yes, sir, I'll let them know to keep the guards on alert and to question the workers," Feldman confirms.

***

The convoy of three trucks pulls out of the abandoned warehouse and starts on the road toward the mining camp. As planned, the first two trucks each contain a four-wheel all-terrain vehicle and a garrison of armed, freshly evolved men. The third truck is transporting the four-wheeler with a pickup-style bed on the back. It is already loaded with a wooden crate strapped down with cables. Anubis is in the ATV's driver's seat, and Isis is riding shotgun.

Isis pulls out a gun clip to check it and reassure herself and slides it back into place. "You know, this reminds me of when we first met," she says, slipping the gun back into its holster and glancing over at him. "Not the contras story, but our real first meeting in Cairo."

"But I love the contras story," he says with a grin. "And it always pisses Osiris off when we tell it."

"I do like that part too," she agrees, tilting her head back dramatically.

"I guess it kind of does," Anubis replies as he runs a toothpick through his teeth.

Isis shifts to check her other gun. "You and Brutus were trying to rob Ra's warehouse in Cairo," she says with a hint of nostalgia in her voice.

"Yep," he says, dragging the toothpick from his mouth. "I remember the first time I laid eyes on that crazy Afro of yours."

"The looks on your faces when you came into my art gallery and could hear my cells buzzing from across the room," she says with a laugh.

He laughs with her. "It was one thing to find out that you were evolved and quite another when we learned just how insane you were."

"Upstanding art dealer by day, privateer thief by night," she says wistfully. "Those were the days ...."

He shakes his head at the memory. "We just needed some intel. We had heard that after Berlin fell, Ra and Alexander raided Hitler's African storage facilities and scored big ... so many relics and art pieces that the Nazis stole during the war. We wanted a piece of that before they moved it out of the country."

"And I wanted in on the job the moment I realized what you were planning. Though, I was so newly evolved I had much to learn.

Only thing I knew for sure was I was done thieving in abandoned mines after my partner and I encountered the virus." She pauses a moment. "Poor guy wasn't as lucky as me. I had to leave him in the sand for the vultures to finish off," she adds, stone faced.

Anubis glances over at her, then gently kicks her foot. "I guess we weren't as clever as we thought, though. Thi Thi nearly took my head off with her staff in that warehouse fight," he says, rubbing his jaw.

She kicks him back. "Ha, you looked so funny with your jaw broken," she says. "I still think we could have gotten away if Bru hadn't given up."

"The bloke's heart wasn't in it. It's as simple as that." Anubis traces the spokes of the DNA strand tattooed on his arm with a line of spit from his toothpick, rewetting it every few seconds.

"He nearly got us killed," she says flatly.

"Yeah." He grimaces. "I think I like the contras story better. With a little luck, we may get a chance today to repay the favor."

She smiles. "I gave him a good lick on the shoulder in Charleston. It would be nice to have another crack at him and his little Latina firecracker. Winner takes all, this time."

He shoots her a look. "If they get in our way, we take them out," he says firmly. "If not, we get the job done and hit the road. Understood?"

Suddenly, the driver of the truck slams his fist against the back of the cab three times.

"It's game time, love, give us a kiss for good luck."

She grabs him by the neck and pulls him in for a passionate kiss, giving his lip a tug as she pulls away. "Let's go, babe," she says, her hands held out in front of her, fingers fluttering with excitement.

CHAPTER 30

"The Evos trucks are approaching the gate!" says Carson, his adrenaline starting to kick in. "Send word to Philippe. Everyone, be ready to go!" He crisply barks out his orders.

Decklan and Lauren exchange nervous glances. "Who could have imagined two mild-mannered scientists would be entering a firefight in a South American jungle?" Dek whispers to her.

Lauren is laser focused, ignoring his comment. "Be ready," she whispers back to him and the men behind them.

***

The men guarding the front of the camp can hear the trucks thundering down the dirt road before they can actually lay eyes on them.

"Something's coming," one of them says. "Are we expecting any deliveries?"

"No, not that I'm aware of," the other guard responds, pulling out his radio. "Let me call it in."

Before he can do more than tap a button, the first truck comes into view. The driver steps on the accelerator, heading right for them. One guard is able to jump out of the way, but the truck is on the other one too fast. As he tries to unholster his pistol, the truck knocks him ten feet into the jungle. Then the passenger of the second truck opens fire, riddling the other guard with bullets and alerting the rest of the men in the camp.

In the back of the third truck, Isis's eyes light up at the sound of gunfire. Anubis starts the engine of the four-wheeler as she pulls her pistols out in front of her.

The first two trucks go barreling into the camp, slamming into some of the smaller vehicles and incapacitating them. The truck in front screeches to a halt twenty feet in front of the main command post. The minute it stops, the guards surrounding the post lace the cabin of the truck with bullets, killing both the driver and passenger.

The second truck pulls up ten feet behind the first, using it as a shield and setting up positions to return fire. Two ramps descend from the backs of all three trucks, and the four-wheelers roar to life. Zipping down the ramps, they tear a path through the heavy equipment lining the sides of the road. Men pour out of the trucks, flooding the left side of the road and concentrating their fire on the right side of the command hut.

Men on both sides are falling fast as the last truck pulls up behind the other two, angling its back toward the right side of the road. Anubis and Isis speed down the ramp on the four-wheeler containing the bomb. Their truck driver and passenger lay down cover fire to allow their escape, and they accelerate quickly.

Decklan and Lauren's group of about ten erupt out of the jungle on the right side of the road just as Anubis bypasses the heavy machinery. They weren't expecting Anubis to be coming their way and are taken by surprise as Isis shoots down the man standing next to Dek, the man's blood splattering across Dek's face. Dek throws himself on the ground for cover as Isis lets out a feral scream and keeps firing.

A second man falls, and this time Lauren is diving to the ground. Her gun ready, Lauren empties a magazine at the four-wheeler as it races off toward the dig site, bouncing on the rough terrain. Most of her shots hit the four-wheeler, but a steel grate on the bed absorbs most of the bullets. "Shit!" she yells and quickly talks into her communicator. "Anubis and Isis are through."

Getting back to her feet, Lauren is only up for a second before more bullets are fired her way. The driver and passenger from the third truck have found cover behind the heavy machinery and have Lauren and Dek's team pinned down just a few feet out into the open.

Back at Maria's truck, Carson throws his earpiece to the ground. His frustration at being left on guard duty is evident. "What the fuck!" he roars. "How could they just let Anubis through?"

Maria is on the communicator, letting the dig-site team know the score. "They're coming, and they know we're here. Be ready," she says bluntly.

"Where the hell is Philippe?" yells Carson, trying to make sense of all the movement on the satellite footage.

**

At the main compound, Helms's men and Ra's men are at a stalemate, exchanging fire from points of coverage. One of the four-wheelers is in flames at the edge of the jungle, and the other is parked behind the main barracks, sheltered from the main hut's defenses. Helms is hunkered down behind his desk, clutching a heavy machine gun. Feldman is hiding in one of the side rooms with three guards.

"Hey! Two of you go out the back and around the left side. Go around the trucks and flank them," Helms yells. The men duck down and scurry out the back door, moving away from the main fight. They sneak around, staying low, and watch Decklan and Lauren's group get pinned down. Helms's men nod at each other, then circle out, firing on Ra's men. The passenger, who was out front, is hit, and that forces the driver to back off of his position.

Dek and Lauren jump up and come running forward, eager to get cover. Two of Ramon's men are with them. The rest fell in battle or hightailed it out of there when the bullets started flying. The foursome stands face-to-face with Helms's men.

"Who the fuck are you guys?" one of Helms's men asks as they all duck behind the cover of a large drill truck.

"We're here to help," says Dek matter-of-factly.

As more gunfire erupts, Helms's men don't have time to question them. With a swift nod, one of them says, "We are trying to flank them. Most of their forces are attacking the other side of the camp."

"A four-wheeler tore down the path toward the dig site," Lauren says. "Do you have guards down there?"

The man pauses briefly, wondering how she knows about the dig. He responds as vaguely as he can. "It should be well defended, but nothing has been mined yet, so there's nothing to steal."

"Fuck," Dek curses as they hear a barrage of gunshots and men screaming.

"We have to move," a Helms man says. They begin to creep carefully along the back of the large vehicles, darting across an open space between two drilling rigs. One of Ramon's men, who is just behind Dek, is shot down as he takes his first step into the open area.

"Sniper!" the other Helms man yells as they all duck for cover. "I think he's on top of the cab of the truck."

"I got him," says Dek. He uses the back of the large driller and quickly scampers to the top, maximizing all of his evolved speed and agility. He quickly achieves the high ground. "Cover fire!"

They all start firing at the sniper's position, forcing him down.

Dek is easily able to pick him off from his higher vantage point. "Got him," he says, swinging down and jumping his way to the ground like a gymnast. "Now what's the plan?" he asks.

The Helms men eye Dek's quickly depleting team for a moment. "From what I've observed, these guys are not well trained," one of them says slowly. "Their positions are not well thought out. If we come at them from behind, I think they'll fold."

Lauren nods. "Okay, you lead."

CHAPTER 31

As they approach the dig site, Anubis gives Isis a quick look and then hard cuts the steering wheel to the left, veering off the path and crashing through the woods. Using the momentum of the sharp turn, Isis leaps from the passenger side, lands in the middle of the path, and runs into the jungle off to the right.

Anubis bursts through into the clearing, driving around the outside rather than into the middle of the dig-site area. This sharp lateral movement causes the guards stationed there to shift their positions to get an angle of fire. They had set up defensive positions focused on the opening of the road from the camp, expecting the infiltrators to come through there. Their guns erupt, chasing Anubis as he speeds around the outside of the clearing. They are all firing off to their left as Isis emerges from the jungle growth like a cheetah, fast, silent, and deadly. She has their positions identified as they send a stream of bullets after Anubis. She has every one of them neutralized before Anubis has gone halfway around the clearing. He pulls to a stop as the machine-gun fire ceases. Looking across the clearing to Isis, he smiles triumphantly.

"Yeah, babe ...." Isis yells back, her voice trailing off abruptly as she sees the hulking form of Brutus erupting from the jungle. He grabs Anubis with both hands, ripping him out of the four-wheeler before he can even grab for his gun.

Off to the left of Brutus, a rip of gunfire ignites. Two bullets hit Isis in the right shoulder as she dives for cover.

Cleo and Thi Thi run out from their point of jungle cover. Thi Thi is sprinting like a gazelle; Cleo is laying down a continuous stream of cover fire, keeping Isis pinned to the ground. As they cross the clearing, Brutus holds Anubis's lanky form with his left hand and lets fly a right-handed punch to the head. The force of the punch throws Anubis's body back against the side of the four-wheeler, and the impact rocks the vehicle.

Anubis, stunned for a moment, tries to clamor over the back of the four-wheeler. Brutus, surprisingly fast for his size, is quick to grab him again before he can get to a weapon. He lifts him up and throws Anubis across the clearing about ten feet.

"Good to see ya, mate," he says, walking after Anubis, who is now sprawled out on the ground. "I don't think I need you getting hold of any of the weapons you undoubtedly have hidden on that ride."

Cleo stops shooting as Thi Thi, carrying a wooden staff, closes in on Isis. Isis turns to shoot the minute that Cleo lets up, but it's too late. Thi Thi swings the staff with the speed of a viper, sending both guns flying from Isis's grasp. The next strike lands directly on her injured shoulder, causing Isis to scream out in pain.

"I've got her," says Cleo, walking up beside Thi Thi, submachine gun trained on Isis. "Just stay down, chica. It's over."

Brutus draws his gun and aims it at the crumpled form of Anubis, lying face down in the dirt. "Like the lady said, stay down, mate. It's over."

***

With their zero-hour plan in place, Dek, Lauren, and Alejandro—Ramon's guy—break off from the Helms guards and sprint from the back side of the truck into the jungle. They work their way around, moving quickly through the overgrowth and circling behind the still-functioning four-wheeler. They slow their pace and draw their guns as they approach. They can see the four-wheeler; one man is still sitting in the driver's seat as another man is keeping them covered, randomly firing on the main hut from around the bunkhouse. There is a third man who is on the far side of the four-wheeler from their position, and he seems to be working on something on the ground.

"We got them," Dek whispers as they near the edge of the jungle canopy.

"I can't see what the guy is doing on the ground," Lauren whispers back.

"Let's go! If we wait, they could gain the advantage," Alejandro says and leads the way.

They emerge from the jungle with guns blazing. The driver and the man at the side of the bunkhouse are hit almost immediately and slump to the ground, but one of their hastily fired shots takes down Alejandro. The man on the back side of the vehicle stands up, and they can now see what he was working on. He starts to raise an RPG, pointing it at them. Dek is first to make it out and turns sharply. Firing his gun with his left hand, he grabs Lauren and takes her to the ground, obscuring her from the shot. One of Dek's bullets grazes the shooter on his left side as he heaves the RPG onto his right shoulder. The shock of the hit causes the shooter to fire the grenade before it is fully raised, right into the passenger side of the four-wheeler. The vehicle erupts into a colossal fireball, the shock of which knocks Decklan off of Lauren and stuns all three of them.

The smoke starts to clear, and Dek is groaning as he rolls over, distantly hearing Lauren's voice. "Dek, Dek, wake up."

He looks up and sees one of Helms's men standing over him. "It worked," Dek says, sighing in relief.

"Um, Dek, he's pointing that gun at us," she says, pushing on his shoulder.

He quickly returns to consciousness. "Shit!" he says, raising his hands.

"Get up, you two," the man says, kicking at Dek's feet. "Yes, our little plan worked. But you just randomly show up to help us?" he says sarcastically. "And you know a little too much about this camp, so we're taking you to the boss. He'll determine what to do here."

Lauren helps Dek to his feet. The back of his shirt is still smoking from shielding her from the blast. They walk up to the command hut, parts of it riddled with bullet holes. Two other men are standing by the main door, and a heated discussion is going on inside as they enter.

"We have to get the injured out of here or they'll die," a tall, thin man is imploring the larger man sitting at a desk.

Both men stop talking, their attention drawn by Dek and Lauren entering the room.

"What on earth are you doing here?" asks the taller man, looking at them in shock.

The man behind the desk just smiles knowingly.

"I don't think we know you," replies Dek. He glances back and forth between the men and Lauren, before settling on her. "Do we?"

"I know him." Lauren points to Feldman. "Well, maybe not his name, but he is the man who initially interviewed me to take on the sample-testing job in Madison."

"Decklan Thomas and Lauren Summers," Helms says. "I never thought I would actually meet you in person. I must say that we massively underestimated you. To have you show up here, attacking this facility in the jungles of Ecuador, I am truly shocked."

"Sorry, but who are you?" asks Decklan.

"My guess is this is Richard's stepfather, Mr. Helms of Helms Chemical. Am I correct?" says Lauren.

"Very good, Dr. Summers, but could you ever guess what an *unbelievable* pain in the ass you two have been over the past months?" He gestures to Feldman. "Take these two men and get the wounded in a truck to the hospital in Nueva Loja, then alert the police that we have been attacked here and will need assistance."

He looks at the two other men in the room. "You two will stay here with me to sort this out."

Feldman looks around briefly, still a bit shell-shocked, then quickly leaves the hut to help the injured.

"We were working with your men here to stop the group attacking you," says Dek, looking at the man who brought them in, for confirmation.

"It's true, sir, they took out the men behind the barracks who were about to fire an RPG into this building," he confirms.

Helms looks at them, a little confused by this information. "So you are here to help me? That sounds a lot like what I heard from this man earlier." He motions to the other guard standing off to the side, near a small closet. The man opens the closet and drags out Philippe. His face is beat up, his mouth is gagged, and his hands are tied behind his back.

"I can see by your reaction that you know this man," continues Helms. "I was able to pick him out trying to sneak in with our regular workers. He also claimed to be here to try and stop someone from harming us, and as near as I could see, he wasn't giving me any signs that he wasn't telling the truth."

"Yes, it's true, we heard of a group planning to attack this location. We came here to help you stop them," says Lauren.

One of the trucks outside fires up and pulls off, presumably with the injured men. This momentarily distracts the Helms men, giving Philippe a fraction of a second to make eye contact with Lauren and show her he is free of his bonds. The look on his face promises retribution in short order. Lauren subtly taps her foot in acknowledgment.

"Look, Mr. Helms, none of this needed to happen at all," Lauren says with fury in her voice. "If this guy"—she jerks her thumb at Dek—"hadn't busted into my lab and messed up my testing—"

"What the hell are you bringing that up for?" Dek yells, raising his hands in frustration.

Before he can say another word, Lauren and Philippe move in lightning-fast sync, each taking out the guards that were standing next to them. They pick up the guards' guns, smiling at each other.

"Okay," Lauren says, breathing heavily. "We're in control now."

"We are all getting out of here and shutting down this dig site," says Philippe. He puts a hand on Helms's shoulder, signaling him to get up.

Dek steps back, shocked at the rapid shift in room dynamics. "Holy shit, what was that?"

Lauren looks down at the unconscious guard lying at her feet before responding. "Philippe and I practiced different escape scenarios while you were with the Evos."

Helms glances up at this statement and smiles to himself. With speed equal to what was just on display, he reaches across his body with his right hand and grabs Philippe's hand in a viselike grip. Helms thrusts his left hand up and through Philippe's elbow, driving it completely in the wrong direction. Philippe screams in agony. Helms jumps up and throws Philippe across the desk and through the window.

In utter shock, Lauren starts to raise the gun that she picked up from the guard. Helms puts his foot up on the desk and shoves it forcefully across the room. It flies at Dek and Lauren, causing both to jump out of the way as it crashes into the fallen guard. Helms pulls out a pistol and takes cover in the closet as Lauren braces herself over the side of the desk, aiming her rifle at the closet. Dek peeks over the other side of the desk.

"My god! What was that?" he whispers over to Lauren.

"I think our friend Mr. Helms may have had contact with the virus at some time before you or me. In fact, I would guess that this whole mining mission may be for the virus and not the radiated metal," she says quietly, keeping her aim tight on the closet. "Is that right, Helms?" she yells. "I know you can hear our whispers."

"I always liked you, Summers. That is why it pained me so to green-light your termination. Sometimes you can be too smart for your own good," Helms says from the closet.

"When did it happen? How long have you been planning this?" asks Dek. He can just see a small part of Helms's body from his angle of view.

"Years ago, right here in fact. I am the reason that the locals say that this land is poison. I was leading a crew looking for rare chemical components. My group found a man who was boring out metal samples from deep in the ground. We found his dead body and the few samples he had next to him. The next morning when the sun rose, I evolved and the other men died," he boasts, as if he were glad to finally tell his story.

"You're a pathetic human being," Lauren says with disgust. "So what, your plan is to just sell evolution to the highest bidder?" She signals to Dek that she doesn't have a shot. He signals back, and she gives him a nod.

"It's going to feel so good putting a bullet in each of your heads," says Helms, the floor squeaking slightly as he shifts his weight, preparing to make a move.

Lauren fires off two shots into the doorframe of the closet, forcing Helms to recoil. She slides the gun across the surface of the desk, toward Dek, and ducks.

Helms extends his gun from the closet door, firing at Lauren's position, splintering the side of the desk. Dek catches the gun at his side of the desk and puts two bullets into Helms's side, causing him to drop his gun and lunge for the back door. Dek fires his last three shots at Helms.

CHAPTER 32

Outside of the main command hut, Philippe is struggling to get up, his right arm severely broken. He starts to crawl toward one of the vehicles to use as a brace. More gunfire breaks out inside the hut, and he sees a bloody Mr. Helms throwing himself over the back deck railing, followed by a few more bullets.

"I hope that I am not too late," he thinks as he struggles to run off through the woods toward Maria's communication truck.

Maria is frantically typing on one of her keyboards in the comm truck as Carson stares at the satellite feed from the dig site.

"Oh my god. I think we got them," he yells. "It's hard to tell, but I think we captured both Isis and Anubis. They are away from the bomb, and it is not even close to the actual dig site," he says excitedly.

"I got it," she says and spins in her chair to face him.

"What ...?" he asks, glancing over at her. At the last second, he registers that she is holding a gun. Carson looks at her in confusion, and she shoots him in the chest, the bullet throwing his body against the side of the truck.

***

At the dig site, the crate on the back of the four-wheeler begins to beep. Keeping his gun trained on Anubis, Brutus walks to the back of the vehicle and finds the bomb timer counting down.

"Er, we have a problem here," he yells across the clearing. "Shut it off, you piece of shit," he says as he grabs Anubis by the shirt.

Isis takes advantage of the distraction and pulls a knife from her boot, throwing it right into Cleo's side.

Cleo screams and drops to one knee. Isis spins on the ground, avoiding the strike of Thi Thi's staff. She kips herself up and kicks Thi Thi back away from her. Then Cleo fires her gun, silencing Isis with three shots to the chest. Her body falls limply to the ground.

Thi Thi rushes to help stop Cleo's bleeding just as Anubis kicks Brutus hard in the groin, causing Brutus to release his hold and fold over on his knees.

"Thanks for the distraction, love," Anubis says as he jumps up and runs off, diving into the jungle foliage at the nearest side of the clearing.

Brutus struggles to his feet, panting. "Somehow he has activated the bomb," he says when he reaches the women. "We have less than three minutes."

"Take her and go!" yells Thi Thi, sprinting back for the four-wheeler.

Brutus picks up Cleo in his arms and starts running back down the road toward the camp, glancing back to see if Thi Thi is coming. He watches Thi Thi slide across the front seat, grab the steering wheel, and accelerate in the opposite direction of the camp, mowing through the jungle overgrowth as quickly as the vehicle will go.

***

Carson is breathing shallowly as he bleeds out, lying against the side of the comm truck, while Maria watches the satellite feed closely, tracking the events at the dig site as they are unfolding. "Goddamnit, Thi Thi!" she says, rushing back to her other computer. "I guess full manual detonation will have to be the way," she says to Carson, smiling back at his fading consciousness.

Before she can type two words, the door of the communication truck bursts open, and Philippe staggers in. He shoots her three times in the chest, and her lifeless body falls next to her computer, the cursor poised over the detonate icon.

Philippe rushes to Carson, trying to help stop the bleeding as best he can with a severely broken right arm. "Stay with me, bro. Focus on stopping the bleeding," he says, applying pressure to the wound.

**

Brutus is running full speed as he breaks into the main-camp clearing, carrying Cleo in his arms. "I got you, babe," he tells her as she holds on to him as best as she can.

Dek and Lauren are outside of the command hut looking around, wondering where Philippe is, when they see Brutus.

"Oh shit, Dek, this can't be good."

They both start running.

"Brutus! Over here!" Dek yells, motioning for them to take shelter behind some of the big equipment.

**

Maria must have activated the bomb, Anubis thinks as he easily reorients himself to find the extraction point. She had been feeding them information on the Children for months. Anubis listens for the sound of helicopter blades. *There is no way she would leave us out here.* He can hear a distant sound of a motor coming his direction, but it seems to be coming from the wrong way. Assuming that Maria set a five-minute timer, the bomb should be going off any minute. Just the thought of it gets him to start walking a little farther away from the direction of the dig site.

The sound he was hearing comes flying out of the brush, crashing into the clearing. The four-wheeler, the bomb, and Thi Thi come to a screeching halt about thirty yards from Anubis. Their eyes lock, each shocked to see the other there. Thi Thi gets one last big smile as she realizes where she has ended up and who is here with her at the end.

In the next second, the bomb goes off, destroying a square mile of forest.

CHAPTER 33

The bomb's explosion knocks over most of the buildings in the camp. The heavy digging equipment proves to be some of the best cover against the force of the blast, shielding Dek, Lauren, Brutus, and Cleo from the worst of it.

Dek stands up and looks around as clouds of smoke billow through the camp.

Lauren helps Brutus take care of Cleo's injury. "I've had worse," she jokes, putting on a brave front.

After a few minutes, Maria's communication truck comes rumbling down the road. Philippe is at the wheel. He stops and carefully lowers himself out.

"Are you okay?" Lauren asks, looking at his mangled arm.

"I will be, once it's set back into place," he says soberly. "But Carson is dead. Maria killed him." He pauses and twists his neck with a painful crack. "She activated the countdown on the bomb ... and it seems she was feeding information to the Evos for months."

Slack-jawed, they stare at him in disbelief.

"I got to her before she had a chance to directly detonate the bomb," Philippe adds quietly.

"Thi Thi ..." Brutus begins, then clears his throat. "Thi Thi was able to get the bomb far enough away from the dig site and the camp to save us all from the blast."

"She is truly a hero today," Cleo says, and suggests a quick moment of silence before they leap back into action.

Dek walks around the wreckage as Lauren bandages Philippe's arm.

"Hey, Philippe," Dek calls. "The bomb obviously caused a lot of damage, but do you think it would have been powerful enough to cause the ninth evolution, if it had been placed in the mine?"

Philippe eyes the destruction around them. "These buildings were never built to last forever," he says. "They were just thrown up to temporarily house the mining crews. The ease at which they were knocked over gives the impression that the explosion was more powerful than it actually was." His gaze drifts to the scorched jungle, and he shivers visibly. "Frenchy had long surmised that it would take a nuclear explosion to cause the ninth …. Thankfully, this was definitely not a nuclear explosion."

Dek nods and returns to Lauren's side. She seems lost in thought, jostled back to the present when Dek throws his arm around her shoulder.

Lauren gazes curiously at Philippe. "How did you know?" she asks. "About Maria, I mean … that she was going to double-cross us."

Philippe lets out a long, unhappy sigh. "Urvinder had doubts. She never specifically told me why, just that the communication center could give someone a great opportunity to mess with our plans. I assigned Carson to stay with her as protection, but I didn't think she would do anything with him there. I clearly underestimated her connection to Ra."

"That begs the question," Dek says. "Why would Ra go through all this trouble, sending his best people, to set off a bomb with so little chance of actually having success?"

Brutus is carefully lifting Cleo off the ground to get her repositioned in one of the camp's transport vehicles. She taps Brutus's chest, causing him to stop, and looks at the group wearily.

"When I was a little girl, my friends and I would often use small sleights of hand to make it easier to pick the pockets of travelers," Cleo says. "If we knew that there was going to be a large event with lots of prime pockets to pick, we would create a large distraction, drawing the eyes of many and making it that much easier to accomplish our goals." Her gaze flickers over all of their faces. "Could this be a distraction from the main event?"

Philippe frowns. "Come to think of it, Ra's number one is not here. Our intel said that Osiris was in Ecuador, but I didn't see her."

"Sacrifice a few pawns in a distraction, move to ultimately win the game?" adds Dek.

"But who does Ra have left? He would never do any of his own dirty work," Philippe says.

"Shit," Brutus says. "When did Urvinder first start to doubt Maria's loyalty?"

"Why?" Lauren asks, confused. "Wait, do you think there's a chance Maria wasn't working alone, and Urvinder found out?"

"Urvinder only spoke to me about it just before we left to come here," Philippe says slowly, "right after we heard about Frenchy's—"

"Urvinder may be in trouble," Cleo says.

Silence briefly fills the air while they all digest that.

Brutus hefts Cleo higher in his arms. "If we leave now, we can be home by morning," he says, the urgency clear in his voice.

As the trucks pull away from the disaster scene, Lauren and Decklan can't help wondering what was really accomplished here.

CHAPTER 34

As the sun-cast shadows of the Central African plain begin to shorten, signifying the height of the midday sun, a lone figure sits on a folding chair reading a book. There is a large tent with electronics set up on shaded tables. The blades of a helicopter peek out from twenty yards behind the tent. Despite the heat, the man's chair is set up in the direct sun, just outside of the tent's shaded areas. He reads quietly, waiting for the work to be accomplished. His legs crossed, he taps his foot in nervous anticipation.

He raises his head when he hears the truck. He'd been following the sound of that vehicle since it came into range. It pulls to a stop behind him, about fifty yards from the tent. A smile crosses the man's face as he hears the gentle tapping of a cane on the arid, sun-dried crust of the African earth. He gently closes his book, shuts his eyes, and listens to the slow, methodical tapping as the visitor approaches the tent.

"So, my friend, it looks like the news of my demise did not fool you." Frenchy stands up from his chair and turns to face Urvinder. He is positively beaming, absolutely loving the fact that she is here.

"I would almost think you were calling me home," she replies.

"Yes, yes, this was your home once, was it not? It took me many years to figure out just where on the African continent you had encountered the virus, some one hundred and eighty years ago, I would guess?"

She just stands there looking at him. Knowing him for all these years, Urvinder is well aware that he is dying to tell her everything.

He begins to walk back and forth in front of his chair like a showman. "Well, where would be a better place to start the ninth evolution than the location where the first recorded interaction with the ninth evolutionary virus took place?" He smirks at her continued silence. "I can tell that you would like to know everything. Well, to be honest, I would love to tell you! I've never been a big fan of keeping secrets, but do you know the best part of keeping secrets?" he asks, talking as much to himself as to her. "I get to be the one who finally exposes the truth. But first I have a question for you. How did you know that I wasn't killed by Isis?"

"When Maria first brought up the live footage from the scene where you were killed. That is, before she rewound the time to the point where your car was at the scene. The tire marks from your car were there, but there were no shards of glass on the ground. There was only gravel when Maria's tampered image of Isis shooting you came up; clearly the rear side window was blown out. Where did the glass go ... or was it never there to begin with?"

"Oh my god, that's so good. I guess the devil is in the details. Just like some famous detective from a novel, maybe Sherlock Holmes? I don't know, who's your favorite?" he asks playfully.

"I'll go with Encyclopedia Brown," she says dryly.

"Oh my goodness, you would, wouldn't you," he responds, laughing. "Okay, here's the big one: How did you know that this is where I would be?"

"Let's just put it to your flare for the dramatic."

Frenchy nods, delighted. "Yes, that's me all right."

Urvinder never takes her eyes off him as he continues to pace. "Allow me to ask you a question?"

"Oh, but of course, my friend."

"What is your ultimate plan here, your endgame?"

"I'm *so* glad you asked that," he says excitedly. "We are going to set off a small nuclear bomb in that abandoned mine right over there." He gestures to a hole in the mounded portion of land. "We have already fully examined the site and it is brimming with viral-containing dirt. We have also examined the conditions of the soil above the explosive and feel that it is ideal to allow multiple viral fragments to be blown into the atmosphere." He claps his hands. "When the sun is at its highest point today—allowing for maximum viral activation—the wind conditions will be perfect for carrying the viral particles to every spot on the globe. Well thought out, don't you think, E.B.?"

She exhales a shallow breath, then slowly nods. "Very well thought out, indeed."

"And of course, our new friends came along at the perfect time, setting up a dream scenario in Ecuador that removed most of our, er, obstacles." He grins and backhands a wave at her. "Except for you, of course."

"Do you think that I alone could stop you?" she asks.

"Oh, are you alone? Of course you are," he says, answering his own question. "Can you alone stop me? I don't think so. You see, Urvinder, if anyone in the group was going to figure this out, it had to be you. Having known you for so long, I figured you would come and try to stop me all by your lonesome. You have a way of doing that."

He raises his eyebrows at her silence. "I'll judge by your reticence that I am right. Man, I love it when I'm right."

"Mmm, you do know me well," Urvinder says. "So you and Ra cooked up this little plan together .... Did you keep the rest of the Evos team in the dark?"

Frenchy is practically floating on air as he preens. "Ra and I have been dreaming of this day for decades, ever since we came up with our wonderful little timeline. But this plan is too devious for us. I'll give you one guess who's plan this is?" He looks at her expectantly.

"Was it our dear Ms. O.?" she asks dryly.

He snickers. "Yes, I thought I was good, but you, *you* are good."

"You two deserve each other," Urvinder mutters under her breath.

"Oh, now don't be such a sore loser!" he crows. "You have to give credit where credit's due. Look at all the power she attained? Osiris, who came from nothing, had the brains and the drive in her regular life to propel herself upward and take everything she desired. And then, when she was still hungry, she rolled the dice against the odds—intaking a virus that would more likely kill her than evolve her—and won again!"

"Nice of her to make that same decision for the rest of mankind; no need for them to have a choice in the matter," Urvinder says.

"Leaders will lead, and the rest will follow," he quips.

"Or the rest will die," she shoots back.

Three men come up out of the mine and start walking toward the tent. Frenchy gestures to the helicopter, indicating that it's time to leave.

"Oh my dear Urvinder, it is discussions like these that I will miss the most." He picks up a pistol off the table.

"Stop," she says as he starts to turn the gun on her.

His body is frozen stiff, but his eyes continue to turn toward her, giving her a startled look.

She stands there holding her cane positioned in front of her with both hands, as if trying to decide what should be done with him. Then his body continues to turn until the gun is facing her. He has a confused look on his face as if this is her doing. He fires the gun, shooting her in the stomach.

As she collapses, he guffaws. "Oh my god, that was better than I ever could have believed. You played your part like we had rehearsed it! Oh Urvinder, did you not think that after all these years of watching you do that trick, that I wouldn't know it was coming?"

"It took me many years, but I did figure out that by expanding the magnetic fields of our organs, we're able to scramble the magnetic fields of others, effectively paralyzing them. Once I solved that little puzzle, it was fairly simple to devise a counter to it."

He begins to pick up his things. "The look on your face as I kept turning!" He hoots. "Oh my god … priceless. That is why, my friend, I knew you would come unarmed … so confident that you could just freeze me—predictable and hilarious!"

He starts to walk toward the helicopter, whose blades are now spinning, then turns back to look at her. "You should thank me, you know. You were born here, and now you'll die here. But before you bleed out, you'll live to see the start of the ninth. Farewell, my friend."

Frenchy gets into the helicopter and buckles himself in. Over the sound of the blades, he yells to the pilot, "We need to get clear of the blast radius before I can set this off."

When they get about forty feet above the ground, Frenchy peers outside the window and can still see Urvinder lying on the ground. Suddenly, the helicopter starts to lean to the side. "What the hell's going on up there!" he screams to the pilot.

The helicopter jerks again and starts to nosedive.

Frenchy unbuckles and lurches forward, grabbing the pilot's arm. "What's wrong with you!" he yells. A look of shock crosses his face as he realizes that the pilot is being frozen by Urvinder on the ground. The helicopter tilts nose down, causing it to fly laterally. Before he has a chance to grab the detonator, the helicopter crashes into the ground nose first, exploding into a ball of flame, its momentum carrying it almost one hundred yards from Urvinder when it finally hits.

Urvinder's head falls back on the ground, a tear dripping down her cheek. She knew he would likely have a counter to her paralyzing skill. She also knew his pride would keep him from finishing her off before his victory was complete. He would have no wish to die here with her, so he would have to have an escape route. Her plan the whole time was to stop that escape. She is glad to die here in the place of her birth; she just hates that by causing the paralysis of the pilot, she had to relive the most horrible experience of her life in her last minutes.

CHAPTER 35

On a private jet, having just departed from the airport in Quito, two old friends are enjoying a drink and conversation.

"Well, it's been a long time coming. Are you ready to take the next step?" asks Alexander, gently rotating his brandy on ice.

"Yes," Victor says immediately, but then pauses. Allowing a smile to cross his face, he adds, "I guess when you meet that midpoint age, around one hundred and thirty or so, you need to look for other challenges in life."

Alexander smiles. "Or else life just gets boring in your hundred and fifties."

"May I ask maybe an obvious question? What made you come around to my way of thinking on this matter?" Victor asks with a knowing look in his eyes.

Alexander looks at Victor and sighs. "I don't know that I was ever one hundred percent against you. I just enjoyed being evolved and having a group of special people to enjoy the world with. The idea of it ending and not being able to spend time with the person I'd like to spend time with became increasingly unpleasant. I was never in denial of the ninth; I just wasn't in a hurry for it."

"I see. So you have reconciled with the person in question?" Victor asks with a skeptical tone.

"I believe that we have. Concessions had to be made, but I guess we shall see."

Victor nods and glances out the window. Changing the subject, he says, "This will be a colossal task, keeping this world together through the changes that are ahead. Do you have all of the necessary pieces in place? Are they active and aware the time is near?"

"Yes, I have been working nonstop over the past week." Alexander uncrosses his ankles and sits up straighter. "I have evolved people in every major government in the world, ready to step in with proper guidance once the ninth has begun. At least two in every nuclear country. We can't have the world end as it takes its first steps into the future."

"It was a pity to lose so many along the path to get here, but their sacrifices will not be in vain," Victor says.

They pause a moment to silently toast their fallen comrades.

A door at the back of the plane opens and Osiris walks down the center aisle wearing a red dress and carrying a black clutch, her hair loose and flowing over her shoulders. She looks like a model slinking down the catwalk.

She stops and pours herself a brandy before joining the two men.

"You look refreshed and as beautiful as ever," Victor says as she takes a seat next to him, across from Alexander.

"It felt so good to get in a shower and freshen up."

"That is a beautiful dress," states Alexander, holding eye contact for an extra second.

"Thank you both for the lovely compliments. Now, what are we discussing?"

"Mainly plans for the future," replies Alexander.

Victor nods in agreement.

"How are things going in Africa?" she inquires.

"You were right, my dear. It seems that Frenchy encountered our dear Urvinder," says Alexander.

"And how is he faring in that confrontation?" she asks casually.

"Apparently, not well," replies Alexander. "His helicopter crashed before he could detonate the bomb." He shakes his head grimly.

"That fool," she says, sitting back in her chair and crossing her legs. "Where does that leave us?"

"That leaves us with this." Alexander reaches down beside his chair and lifts up a briefcase. He flips in some code numbers and opens it up, removing what looks like a drone controller.

She smiles at his ingenuity. "Is that a satellite remote detonator?"

"Yes, it is," Alexander replies, pulling up two antennae from the base.

"Will it work up here?" she asks eagerly.

"Yes, it will."

They sit silently watching Alexander prepare the device. "It's armed and ready. Would you like to do the honors, old friend?" he asks Victor, handing him the detonator.

"Thank you." Peering down at it in his lap, Victor fully takes in the moment. He shoots a meaningful look, first at Osiris and then at Alexander, then says, "For the future of humanity ..."

***

Urvinder hears the bomb activation as she lies bleeding on the ground. She knew they would never just leave it up to Frenchy. She looks up to the sky one last time before being consumed by a flash of light and burst of heat. A large mushroom cloud erupts, looming over the African plain and signifying the start of a new age.

***

Victor takes a deep breath and gently sets the device down next to his chair. "It is done."

They all lean forward and clink their glasses.

Their phones begin going off, signifying world knowledge of at least the explosion. Osiris reaches down and retrieves her clutch. Victor looks down at his phone screen, not noticing Osiris is not removing her phone from her purse but a six-inch dagger. She moves with speed and precision as she drives the knife up under Victor's chin, burying the blade to the hilt. She looks him in the eye as the life bleeds out of him.

"Thank you, my love, for allowing him his moment," says Alexander. "Now, we have a lot of work ahead of us."

She removes the knife and wipes the blade off on Victor's pants. "The king is dead; long live the queen."

EPILOGUE

Five-year anniversary of the release of the ninth evolutionary virus "Pull over here. We can walk the rest of the way," Decklan says. He reaches over the seat of the cab to hand their driver a tip.

Lauren looks over and gives him an agreeable nod, pulling her attention from the bustling streets of New York City. She is amazed that even after the evolution took over half of the population, the streets of New York are still bustling.

Dek takes her hand as they proceed down the street. "I was looking over a map on the flight here … we are pretty close to the hotel where the meeting is. I thought it might be nice to walk the last little bit and get a close-up look at the New York Silo before it's shut down."

"I do too," replies Lauren. "I've only seen it depicted in videos on my phone."

They turn at the next corner and Central Park comes into view. In the middle of the park is a large beam of light that extends from the ground up as high as their evolved eyes can see. They can clearly make out the rings of the silo maintaining the integrity of the beam as it reaches beyond the atmosphere.

"I read all about it on the plane," Lauren begins excitedly. "The silo project was designed by Ra in anticipation of the ninth evolution." She starts rapidly pointing things out to Dek, barely allowing herself a breath. "A series of giant rings with a diameter about one hundred yards have a seating ring embedded in the ground that serves as the base and stabilizer. Look there—about ten feet off of the ground—is an incinerator ring, which uses high-intensity heat rays to break down any matter that is transferred through it. There, those ten stabilization rings extend up through the sky. The magnets in those thin metallic rings rotate, causing a whirlwind that acts like a vacuum, pulling organic material up the silo and through the incinerators before it exits our atmosphere and extends into space."

"Ra's solution to the mass casualties that the ninth evolution would create," Dek murmurs, glancing around in awe. "The engineering involved is absolutely crazy."

She nods. "Apparently, he commissioned the construction of thirteen units three years prior to the release of the virus. The units were dispersed around the world in high-population sites to allow for mass cremations without the total pollution of our atmosphere. He counted on the vastness of space and the flow of solar currents to move the ashes away from Earth." Still staring up at the silo, she adds, "I never actually got to meet him, but it's clear he was a next-level thinker."

"Well, I did meet him. Great mind, but a huge narcissist. Not your type," Dek says, smiling.

Dek is bumped into and jostled as groups of people head toward the large gathering in the park. Tonight is the night when the silos around the world will be decommissioned, signifying the end of a worldwide mourning period over the loss of billions of lives.

"Come on, Dek, we've got to keep moving if we want to get to the meeting site before all the excitement begins," Lauren says, taking the lead and pulling him forward.

They break away from the main flow of people, continuing along the outside of the park to a hotel located about a block from the park's main entrance. They are allowed into the lobby after an intense verification process. At the main desk, the clerk gives them key cards to a room overlooking the park and the main area of the night's festivities.

"You guys are going to have the view of the night," says the clerk. "I think a few of your friends are already up there. Enjoy."

Dek and Lauren exchange looks as they turn and walk to the elevator.

Dek pushes the up button and glances at her cautiously. "It's been a while since we've seen any of the Children. Are you ready for this?"

Lauren's silent for a moment before admitting softly, "I think we all needed some space to come to grips with our failure. I mean, we thought we had succeeded, only to find out that we were all fooled on so many levels."

"Do we even know who we're meeting here?" Dek asks as they enter the elevator.

"I would guess most of the old crew. The only message I got was from Alexander. 'It's important that we all be here, and more would be revealed, blah blah,' " she says.

He smiles and nudges her with his elbow. "I'm not sure that we should be trusting Alexander on any level," Dek says slowly. "The way that he so quickly got on board with Osiris's plans for the world has to make you wonder: Was he working with Osiris and Ra, maybe the whole time?"

She shrugs. "From what I've been able to follow on the news, Alexander and Osiris have been the keys to stabilizing the world's transition after the evolution. Aside from a few countries falling into complete disarray, the people that Alexander had in place inside the most powerful countries of the world managed to stop full-scale breakdown."

The doors open onto their floor, and Dek points down the hall. "It looks like the clerk was right. We are going to have front-row seats for the decommissioning of the silo," he quips.

They pause outside the room, taking a deep breath before sliding their key card into the lock. The lights in the room are off as they enter. The main window's shades are pulled open, allowing the rays of the evening sun to peek in around the edges of a hulking figure standing at the window.

Brutus turns around slowly as they enter the main living area. "How're you blokes doin'? It's been a minute, hasn't it?" he says with a slight smile.

"Brutus!" Lauren rushes over to give him a hug. "It's so good to see you. How are you?" she asks, pulling back to look up at him.

"I'm a bit better now, seeing you two," he replies, smiling down at her and then offering a hand out to Dek.

He shakes Dek's hand, then pulls him in for a group hug. "It seems like a lifetime since we all split up after the ninth."

"It's good to see you," says Dek. The big man's arms almost squeeze the air out of him.

"Is Cleo here?" asks Lauren, taking a minute to look around the large and lavish hotel suite.

"No, I'm afraid not." He looks down at the ground. "She lost a lot in the ninth—not that everyone didn't lose a lot—but I guess she didn't do so good with it. She was so distraught, she ended up finding solace with the religious group, the Survivors."

"They affiliated with the TWR religious group?" asks Dek. "I think I saw some of their signs on the trip over from the airport."

"Yeah, the Survivors is the South American version of Those Who Remain, here in the US," Brutus replies.

"Hmm," Lauren says carefully. "Their beliefs are quite contrary to the systems of government that Alexander and Osiris currently have in place to control the world's peace and stability ...."

"Very contrary," Brutus says, peeking back over his shoulder toward a stage that was erected just outside the edges of the silo. "They are basically on the edge of a violent conflict, with the strength of the beliefs on each side."

"I must admit that I am not up to speed with regard to this conflict," Dek admits. "I really didn't think there would be anything more to fight about after the revelations of the ninth."

"I guess it has more to do with how you look at what happened during the ninth," Brutus explains. "Some people look at it as a purely scientific next leap in the evolution of mankind, and others look at it like a form of exodus, a reaping of the nonbelievers before the path to salvation is opened to the chosen."

"Think of it this way, Dek," Lauren begins, "Osiris wants to further the space program she implemented immediately after the silos went operational, but the TWR think it's time for prayer and contemplation. They think it is wrong to look to explore a new frontier, and that glory over God could bring more sorrow."

Before they can continue the conversation, they hear a key card unlocking the door. They watch as a young man walks in. He has deeply tanned skin and a curly mop of dark hair falling over his eyes. He stops and gives them a confused look, like he just walked into the wrong room.

Lauren goes running over to him right away and gives him a big hug, prompting Brutus and Dek to exchange baffled glances.

"It's Philippe!" Lauren exclaims. "Your new look couldn't fool me," she says, teasing his hair.

"Yes, boys, it's me. I couldn't resist changing it up a bit to fool with you." He smiles and walks over to the men.

"Oh shit, mate. You had me with that one," says Brutus, picking him off the ground in a big hug.

"Good to see you, man," says Dek, getting in a smaller hug of his own.

"It's great to see all of you," Philippe says, then breaks away from the group. From a backpack that he was wearing, he removes an old-school cassette tape player with an envelope attached to the bottom of it.

Their attention is briefly pulled toward the window as they hear a cheer go up from the crowd gathered at the park. They can see from their window that the silo has gone dark for the first time. A spotlight shines down on the stage, highlighting the figure of Osiris standing at a podium beginning to talk to the crowd. As she motions toward the silo, its ring lights come to life and the rings begin to descend from the sky back to the base platform.

"Good, I'm not too late," says Philippe, redrawing their attention to the recorder. "Alexander wanted me to play this for you. I don't know what it says. He said that if I can get it started by the time the rings start to descend, the timing should be right."

He presses play, and the tape starts. Alexander's voice fills the room.

"Thank you for coming, my Children of the Sun. I am sorry that it has taken me so long to contact you. There is little time, so I will get to the point. The silos will close tonight, and so closes the period of mourning that has gripped this world since the coming of the ninth. Once again, I must ask for your help. Factions, splintered by opposing views, are growing more and more agitated. I fear a war for the dominant viewpoint is coming, a battle for one group's convictions alone to rule the world. This was something that I believe Victor and Frenchy may have anticipated. I need you to look through their research to hopefully find an answer. We will reconvene upon the completion of these tasks and put the final motions into play. Do not be fooled by what is unfolding before you. If we keep to the plans, we will achieve success. Farewell, my friends, and good luck." The tape goes silent.

"Is that it?" asks Dek, looking at the wheels of the player slowly spinning in silence.

"Did anyone get what it is that we are supposed to do?" adds Lauren. Looking around at the other confounded faces in the room, she guesses no.

"Well, I suppose we could just ask him when he's done with his little show," says Brutus, pointing out the window.

The group moves to peer down at the gathering in the park. Alexander is standing on the stage next to Osiris, just outside of the spotlight. The last of the rings has come down and is gently resting on the stabilization rings. Osiris shouts to the crowd, and the rings all finish their descent by lowering into the ground, flush with the surface. She steps aside, and Alexander steps up to the mic.

"In the center of these great rings of destruction, we will plant peace trees," he says somberly. "And at the site of each silo, these trees will grow and flourish, as will our newly evolved species in the years to come. These sites will become a place of worship and reflection as we continue to heal and move forward." He holds Osiris's hand and confidently raises their arms in the air. Seconds later, a stream of bullets tears through his body, turning the podium into splinters. Screams erupt from the crowd as Alexander's body falls lifeless to the ground.

www.ingramcontent.com/pod-product-compliance
Lightning Source LLC
Chambersburg PA
CBHW031953010726
47493CB00007B/2189